H.I.V.E.

DEADLOCK

OTHER BOOKS BY MARK WALDEN

Earthfall

The H.I.V.E. Series

H.I.V.E. #1:
Higher Institute of Villainous Education

H.I.V.E. #2:
The Overlord Protocol

H.I.V.E. #3:
Escape Velocity

H.I.V.E. #4:
Dreadnought

H.I.V.E. #5:
Rogue

H.I.V.E. #6:
Zero Hour

H.I.V.E. #7:
Aftershock

H.I.V.E.

DEADLOCK

MARK WALDEN

SIMON & SCHUSTER BOOKS FOR YOUNG READERS

NEW YORK LONDON TORONTO SYDNEY NEW DELHI

SIMON & SCHUSTER BOOKS FOR YOUNG READERS
An imprint of Simon & Schuster Children's Publishing Division
1230 Avenue of the Americas, New York, New York 10020
This book is a work of fiction. Any references to historical events,
real people, or real places are used fictitiously. Other names, characters, places,
and events are products of the author's imagination, and any resemblance to
actual events or places or persons, living or dead, is entirely coincidental.
Text copyright © 2013 by Mark Walden
Cover illustration copyright © 2015 by Asaf Hanuka
Originally published in Great Britain in 2013 by Bloomsbury Publishing Plc
First US edition 2015
All rights reserved, including the right of reproduction
in whole or in part in any form.
SIMON & SCHUSTER BOOKS FOR YOUNG READERS
is a trademark of Simon & Schuster, Inc.
For information about special discounts for bulk purchases, please contact Simon &
Schuster Special Sales at 1-866-506-1949 or business@simonandschuster.com.
The Simon & Schuster Speakers Bureau can bring authors to your live event. For
more information or to book an event, contact the Simon & Schuster Speakers
Bureau at 1-866-248-3049 or visit our website at www.simonspeakers.com.
Also available in a Simon & Schuster Books for Young Readers hardcover edition
The text for this book is set in Goudy.
Manufactured in the United States of America
1215 OFF
First Simon & Schuster Books for Young Readers paperback edition February 2016
2 4 6 8 10 9 7 5 3 1
Library of Congress Control Number: 2014938265
ISBN 978-1-4424-9470-1 (hc)
ISBN 978-1-4424-9471-8 (pbk)
ISBN 978-1-4424-9472-5 (eBook)

To the Silver Birch Friday Night Support Club.
You know who you are.

chapter one

"That man is the single most infuriating person on the face of this planet," Maximilian Nero said angrily as he strode out of the restaurant and onto the busy pavement. Around him the crowded Hong Kong street bustled with activity, illuminated by the countless neon signs that hung from every shopfront and doorway. Diabolus Darkdoom followed him out onto the street, handing a wad of banknotes over to the owner, who had run out after them complaining noisily. He caught up with Nero and sighed, shaking his head.

"Can't be built," Nero said irritably. "I'll show him can't be built."

"You did ask his opinion, Max," Darkdoom said. "You can't get angry with him just for disagreeing with you."

"He's only offended because I completed the design myself," Nero said.

"Max, you know I have the greatest respect for your abilities," Darkdoom said, "but even I have to admit that your finished design seems a touch ambitious and he is the most well-respected architect in the business. There aren't many people who can design and build the sort of building that is required in our line of work and your—"

"So you're taking *his* side now, are you?" Nero said.

"Never mind," Darkdoom said, throwing up his hands. "I'm not getting involved. This is between you and him. If you want to build the new facility for H.I.V.E. in an active volcano then that's exactly what you should do. It's your baby."

"If he'd done a slightly better job of hiding the last facility maybe we wouldn't be in this position in the first place," Nero said.

"Maybe, but it might have been more diplomatic not to actually have said that to him," Darkdoom said with a slightly exasperated-sounding sigh. "Then we could have at least finished what was turning out to be an exceptionally good meal."

Nero raised his hand and hailed one of the city's distinctive red taxis.

"Although, at least now I do actually know what happens when an immovable object meets an irresistible force," Darkdoom said under his breath as the cab pulled up and Nero climbed inside.

"Airport, please," Nero said to the driver as Darkdoom sat down beside him and slammed the car door shut. "It's not as if I don't have enough to worry about at the moment, Diabolus. Number One's demanding to know why Overlord's behind schedule and Xiu Mei tells me that they're still months away from activation. It doesn't matter how many times I tell him that it's risky to rush the project, he still insists that it's the future of G.L.O.V.E. Meanwhile, I've got Professor Pike in the other ear telling me that he's working on a similar AI project for the school, but that he's years away from perfecting the behavioral restraints that will make it safe to use and that's why Overlord is too dangerous."

"Max, you're my oldest friend," Darkdoom said, "and I think you're one of the most brilliant men on G.L.O.V.E.'s ruling council, but everybody needs a break sometimes, even you. For goodness' sake, just take a couple of weeks off and go and lie on a beach somewhere."

"I'm sorry, Diabolus," Nero said with a sigh, "I don't mean to moan. It's just that the temporary facilities we're using at the moment are completely inadequate. I need to at least get construction started on H.I.V.E.'s new facility; maybe then I can take a break for a couple of—"

Suddenly, the rear windshield of the taxi exploded in a shower of glass and the driver of the cab slumped forward onto his steering wheel.

"Sniper! Get down!" Nero yelled as the taxi swerved, out of control, into oncoming traffic. He took cover behind the seat as more high-velocity rounds buzzed through the air above them. There was a sickening crunch and the taxi spun around as it made glancing contact with another car. The cab bounced across the pavement as pedestrians scattered in all directions and slammed into the plate-glass window of a storefront. Nero and Darkdoom scrambled out of the wrecked car, knowing that they would be sitting ducks if they stayed inside it. They took shelter behind the wall next to the shattered window as the last of the shop's customers ran past the angrily gesticulating shopkeeper and fled through the back door.

"Are you hit?" Nero asked Darkdoom.

"No, you?"

"No," Nero replied, picking up a piece of glass from the floor. "Did you see where the shooter was firing from?"

"No," Darkdoom replied. "Shots were on a flat trajectory though. He's got to be somewhere at ground level."

Nero held the piece of glass in just the right position to allow him to see a reflection of the chaotic scenes in the street outside the shop. People were running in all directions and the traffic had ground to a halt. There was only one figure that was out of place, somebody dressed in a skintight black outfit and mask who was walking slowly toward the shop with an assault rifle raised to their shoulder.

A split second later there was a sudden muzzle flash and the piece of glass in Nero's hand exploded. Nero snarled in pain as shards of glass buried themselves in his hand.

"Are you armed?" Nero asked, through gritted teeth.

"No," Darkdoom replied, pulling a communicator from his inside pocket. "I'll call for backup."

"They won't get here in time," Nero said, cursing himself for not bringing a weapon. He had known that the man they were meeting for lunch was no threat to them and so he had let his guard down. He realized now that that might have been a fatal error. "We need to move."

Nero ran toward the back of the store with Darkdoom just behind him. He burst through the beaded curtain that separated the front of the shop from the storeroom at the rear, just in time to see the shopkeeper running through a door at the far end of the racked shelving that filled the area.

"This way," Nero said, running toward the door. They ran out into a garbage-strewn alleyway lined with fire escapes and doorways. Nero looked up and down the alley, trying to spot anything that might give them even a slim tactical advantage over whoever it was that was hunting them.

"Here, help me," Nero said, as he closed the shop door behind them and started to push a wheeled dumpster in front of it. He knew it wouldn't stop their pursuer, but it might slow them down. The two men quickly rolled it into position and Nero engaged the brakes on the wheels.

"We need to split up," Nero said after a moment's thought. "Give that assassin two separate targets." He pulled his own communicator from his jacket pocket and activated its homing beacon.

"The backup teams can track us both individually and at least this way one of us will survive if the worst comes to the worst."

Darkdoom frowned, but he knew that there was no point arguing with Nero at a time like this. His friend had always been the superior tactician. Even if he didn't much like the sound of this particular idea, he had to admit that it did make strategic sense.

"Okay," Darkdoom said, nodding down the alleyway. "I'll go this way. Don't get yourself killed, Max."

"I always try to avoid it," Nero said with a crooked smile. "Be careful, we don't know whether we're dealing with a lone hitter or a team yet. There could be more of them out there."

Darkdoom gave a quick nod and ran off down the alleyway. Nero looked up at the fire escape above him. Heading for the rooftops was risky—it would be all too easy to get trapped up there—but that risk was outweighed by the advantages that elevation would give him. He ran to the ladder leading to the steel staircase and climbed quickly up it. He was halfway to the roof when he heard a bang from below him and saw the door to the shop being slowly forced open. He made it up two more flights of stairs before the black-clad assassin shoved the door open wide and walked out into the alley. Nero froze, watching as the figure looked down the alleyway in both directions. With luck, Nero thought to himself, the assassin would choose the wrong direction and give Darkdoom more of a head start.

A moment later the assassin looked straight up at him, raising his assault rifle. Nero bolted up the remaining stairs, taking them two at a time, sprinting for the roof as bullets pinged off the metal around him. The assassin fired just two short bursts before climbing up onto the fire escape, coming after him. Nero reached the top of the steel staircase and ran onto the roof, looking desperately for the best escape route amongst the numerous air-conditioning vents and skylights that surrounded him. Below him, he could hear the assassin sprinting up the metal stairs; Nero knew he only had seconds.

He ran to the far side of the roof and looked down at the four-story drop to the street below. Too far to drop. He heard a noise behind him and turned to see the assassin climbing onto the roof, rifle raised. Whoever they were they had scaled the side of the building in a fraction of the time it had taken Nero. He took a deep breath; he had always known that it might end like this someday, but he wasn't going to give his killer the satisfaction of hearing him beg for his life. The assassin lowered the rifle and then dropped it to the floor, before pulling off the black mask that hid their face. Nero's eyes widened in surprise as the young woman dropped the mask and drew the twin katanas from her back, their silver blades glinting. She could not have been more than sixteen years old, with short black hair, her pale, pretty face betraying no hint of any emotion as she advanced across the rooftop toward him. He had no idea who she was, but there was something hauntingly familiar about her.

"Anastasia Furan sends her regards," the girl said as she approached. "She wanted you to know that this is for Elena."

"I should have killed Anastasia when I had the chance," Nero said, taking a step backward, feeling a grief that he had long hidden washing over him again at the mention of Elena's name. "And now she sends one of her brainwashed children to kill me. I might have known she wouldn't have the guts to face me herself." Nero heard a rumble from the street behind him and glanced over his shoulder as the girl approached, weapons raised.

"Enough talk," the girl said, her voice calm.

"I couldn't agree more," Nero replied. He turned and jumped from the roof, disappearing from view. The girl sprinted to the edge and looked down into the street below.

She cursed under her breath in Russian as she saw Nero kneeling on the roof of the red double-decker tram that was trundling away down the street, picking up speed. She turned, sheathed her weapons, and sprinted along the edge of the roof, gaining slowly on the tram. When she reached the end of the roof she vaulted over the low wall and leaped into the air, landing on top of a lamppost with seemingly impossible agility, before springing onto the roof of a passing truck that was only twenty yards or so behind the tram.

Nero looked back over his shoulder and saw the girl land on top of the truck like a cat. "Impressive," he said under his breath as the girl waited patiently for the truck to close the distance to the tram. Whoever this young woman was, she had obvious talent.

He had heard the stories about the abilities of the Furans' young killers, but this was the first time he had seen them firsthand. He turned and looked ahead of the tram and saw that they were approaching a set of traffic lights that were just turning red. The truck pulled alongside the tram as it slowed to a halt and the girl vaulted onto the other vehicle. Nero sprang to his feet and charged at the girl, slamming into her hard as she landed. They fell onto the roof, grappling with each other. Nero tried to use the advantage that his extra weight and strength gave him to pin the girl down, but she was just too quick. She delivered a swift blow with the heel of her palm to his chin, his head snapping back, and she squirmed out from underneath him. Nero grabbed desperately at the hilt of one of the swords in the crossed sheaths on her back and pulled it free, rolling away from the girl and struggling to his feet as the girl leaped up and drew the other katana, dropping into a double-handed attacking stance. Nero backed away, holding the blade of his weapon in front of him defensively, trying to ignore the pain from the splinters of glass still embedded in his palm. Now the odds were at least slightly more even, he thought to himself.

The girl took three quick strides toward him, her weapon flashing through the air as she advanced. Nero countered the first couple of blows, astonished by the speed and ferocity of the young girl's attack. He knew how to fight with a blade, but all that meant was he knew almost instantly that he was hopelessly outmatched. The girl's blade was like an extension of her body, moving too fast to follow, let alone counter. The tip of her sword scythed across his chest, leaving a deep bloody cut and Nero staggered backward. The girl drew back the sword and struck, the tip of the blade spearing deep into Nero's thigh and he gave a pained gasp as he felt his leg give way beneath him. He fell to one knee as the girl raised the katana high above her head ready to deal a killing blow.

The traffic lights turned green.

The tram lurched forward and for an instant the girl was caught off balance. Nero desperately swept his own blade upward, catching her off guard and leaving a long, deep gash in her cheek. The girl stepped backward, her left hand instinctively flying up to her face as the savage wound began bleeding profusely. Nero flung his sword to one side and threw himself forward with a grunt, trying to ignore the searing pain in his thigh, and tackled the girl, wrapping his arms around her waist. The pair of them flew off the top of the tram, dropping several yards before slamming down on to the roof of a car below. The katana flew from the girl's hand and clattered into the road, the impact stunning her and knocking the air from her lungs. Nero rolled off her and dropped to the ground with a pained gasp. He picked up the girl's fallen sword and turned back to her just as she rolled off the car's roof. He raised the sword quickly, pressing its tip to her throat, sending a drop of blood trickling down her neck. He saw her tense, ready to strike.

"Don't," Nero said. "You may be fast, my dear, but nobody's that fast."

The girl glared back at him, half her face covered in blood, her eyes narrowing.

"You have no idea how fast I am," the girl said. Nero barely even saw her move as her stiffened knuckles struck his wrist, the sword dropping from his numb fingers and into her other hand. She spun the sword, bringing it to Nero's throat as he took a step backward.

"Time to die."

The single shot rang out and the girl slammed back into the ruined car, sliding to the ground with a startled expression on her face. Darkdoom stepped out from behind a nearby van and lowered the assault rifle that she had abandoned just a few minutes earlier on the rooftop, its muzzle still smoking.

"I had second thoughts about the whole splitting-up thing," Darkdoom said, "fortunately for you. The backup chopper's two minutes out. Are you okay?"

Nero gave a nod and kicked the sword away from the girl's hand before kneeling down beside her and feeling for a pulse in her neck.

"Tell the backup team that we have an urgent med-evac," Nero said, applying pressure to the wound in the girl's chest.

"Are you joking?" Darkdoom said as he began to hear the first wails of police sirens in the distance. "She very nearly killed you. Why on earth would you want to save her life?"

"Because this girl was sent by Anastasia Furan, Diabolus," Nero replied, "and she might just be the only person who can help us find her."

☻ ☻ ☻

Nero watched as the nurses transferred the unconscious girl from the wheeled gurney to the hospital bed on the other side of the thickened glass window. They spent a couple more minutes hooking her up to monitors and putting in an IV line before filing out of the room past the two armed guards stationed outside, a heavy steel door sliding shut behind them with a thud. The girl had just returned from emergency surgery and, lying there unconscious with her chest swathed in bandages and a dressing on the vicious wound on her face, she did not look anything like the threat that she quite clearly was.

"How is she, Doctor?" Nero asked as the head of the G.L.O.V.E. medical facility approached.

"Critical, but stable," the doctor replied. "It's a miracle she survived at all. A gunshot wound like that . . . well, let's just say she is stronger than she looks. It will take time for her to recover fully, of course, but I believe her prognosis is good."

"When she is strong enough, I want her transferred to the temporary H.I.V.E. facility," Nero said. "Until then, be extremely careful, Doctor. Keep her restrained at all times and maintain twenty-four-hour surveillance. This particular patient is very, very dangerous."

"Understood," the doctor said with a nod. "Number One wishes to speak with you. You can use the teleconference system in my office if you would like."

"Thank you," Nero said as the doctor gestured to a door at the far end of an adjoining corridor. "That will be all."

Nero looked back through the window as the doctor

walked away and looked again at the girl lying in the bed. There was something about her that he could not put his finger on, something that was telling him that he had to try to help her, despite what she had done.

"You're getting soft, Nero," he muttered to himself, "and one day it's going to get you killed."

He turned away from the glass and headed to the doctor's office. He sat down behind the desk and activated the teleconference system. The screen lit up with the familiar logo of G.L.O.V.E., the Global League of Villainous Enterprise, a closed fist smashing down on a splintering globe with the words "Do Unto Others" beneath it. He punched in the code that would connect him with Number One, the head of G.L.O.V.E.'s ruling council.

"Please confirm identity," a synthesized voice said a few moments later.

"Nero, Maximilian, authorization code sigma nine delta seven," Nero replied. A few seconds later a silhouetted figure appeared on the screen.

"Good morning, Maximilian," Number One said. "I have just finished reading your report on this recent unpleasantness in Hong Kong. If what this girl said is true, it is most disturbing. I had hoped that we had heard the last of the Furans after their disappearance, but unfortunately that does not appear to be the case."

"Indeed," Nero replied. "I have requested a termination

warrant be placed on them. With your permission I would like to carry out the warrant personally."

"I will consider your request," Number One replied. "I am always wary of letting these situations become too personal, Nero, you know that. I am aware of your history with the Furans and I do not want to see a personal vendetta endanger G.L.O.V.E.'s interests."

"You can trust me to handle the matter professionally, sir," Nero replied.

"As I said, I shall consider your request," Number One said. "And what of the girl? Do you believe she will cooperate?"

"I don't know," Nero replied. "She is still recovering from surgery at the moment. It is impossible to say how deeply she was indoctrinated during her training. It may take time to persuade her to give the Furans up."

"There are quicker methods of persuasion, Maximilian," Number One said, "more painful methods."

"I think she could be useful," Nero said, shaking his head slightly. "Let me see if I can turn her; that way we may gain an asset at the same time as ridding ourselves of a threat."

"I leave it to your discretion," Number One said, "but I want results quickly. This was not just an attack on you and Darkdoom, this was an attack on our entire organization. Our retribution must be swift. The girl must tell us what she knows and soon. My patience has its limits, Nero."

Nero knew all too well what happened to anyone who overstepped those limits.

"I will report my progress with her directly to you," Nero replied.

"See that you do," Number One said. "Do unto others."

"Do unto others," Nero replied with a nod and the connection was cut.

A few hours later, Nero walked into the room where the wounded girl lay strapped to the bed. She was conscious now and she glared at him as he approached.

"You should have killed me when you had the chance," the girl said, her voice dripping with venom.

"I still have that option," Nero replied. "I am simply choosing not to exercise it at this precise moment. Now, you know my name, but I do not know yours. What should I call you?"

"My name is Raven," the girl replied, still glaring at him. "And that is all you will get from me."

"Not your codename," Nero said, shaking his head, "your real name. What is it?"

"My name is *Raven*," the girl hissed back at him. "I have no other name."

"Very well, Raven," Nero replied, "I imagine that someone like you must find this kind of incarceration rather boring, so I've brought this." He held up the battered leather-bound book that he was holding. "I'm afraid I can't release your hands, since I suspect that they would end up around my throat. So, I'm going to have to read it to you. I hope you like it, it's one of my favorite novels and my father read it to me when I was young."

"Do what you like," Raven replied with a dismissive sneer. "It makes no difference to me."

"That's exactly what I used to say to my father," Nero replied with a smile, opening the book and turning to the first page. He cleared his throat and began to read.

"*It was the best of times, it was the worst of times . . .*"

Nero looked down into the combat training area and watched as Raven swiftly incapacitated the men around her. It had been three months since her arrival at H.I.V.E.'s temporary facility in the Alps and her recovery from her injuries had been astonishingly quick. The men she was fighting were no ordinary sparring partners. They were some of the very best of G.L.O.V.E.'s special forces operatives and yet they were being systematically humiliated by the teenage girl in the middle of the room. Initially they had attacked individually, obviously feeling that it would be unfair for her to have to take on more than one of them at once, but that restraint had quickly been abandoned. There were more guards stationed around the edge of the area with the prototype Sleeper stun guns that Professor Pike had just developed. The Professor assured him that these new weapons would incapacitate anyone without causing any lasting physical harm. He hoped for the sake of the men in the room that he was right.

"She's remarkable," Colonel Francisco said, as he walked along the balcony toward Nero. "To be honest with you, Max, I wouldn't have believed it if I hadn't seen it for myself. Those are my best men and she's making them look like amateurs."

"Yes, it would appear that my instinct about her potential was correct," Nero replied. "Now all we have to do is work out how to ensure we can safely tap it. That girl has been subjected to some of the most brutal training imaginable, it is a wonder that her mind is still intact." The truth was that it had taken weeks just to persuade her to engage him in conversation. At first she had maintained a defiant silence, but Nero had not been discouraged. Over the past few years, he had trained many children who had been subjected to the worst kinds of brutality and he knew that there was still time to save the girl. At first, he had talked to her about her life before the Furans, growing up on the streets of Moscow and then slowly he coaxed from her details of the torments that she had suffered at the Glasshouse. Slowly he had begun to catch glimpses of the fiercely independent and resourceful young woman that the Furans had tried so hard to suppress. They thought they had broken her, but in truth she had just hidden that part of herself away, deep inside, somewhere they could not reach it.

"She'll be a huge asset if we can trust her," Francisco said, watching as another of his men went flying.

"Agreed," Nero replied, "so perhaps it is time we found out if we can." He turned and walked to the stairs at the end of the balcony. He made his way down onto the training floor and the guards around the edge of the room visibly tensed.

"Gentlemen, you are dismissed," Nero said as he approached the panting men surrounding Raven. There was no disguising the looks of relief on some of their faces as they walked or limped away.

"You did well," Nero said as he approached Raven. "How are you feeling?"

"Out of practice," Raven replied. "Your men are weak."

"I don't think that's true," Nero replied. "It's just that you are unusually strong. Thank you for honoring my request and not seriously injuring any of them."

"The dozen guns pointing at me made it difficult to disagree," Raven replied.

"Indeed," Nero said, glancing at the men around the perimeter of the room. "Perhaps we should remove them from the equation." He turned to Francisco who was still watching from the balcony above. "You and your men may leave, Colonel."

"Are you sure, sir?" Francisco replied with a frown.

"I'm quite certain, thank you, Colonel," Nero replied.

"Understood," Francisco replied, still frowning. "Clear the room."

Raven and Nero watched in silence as the guards filed out, leaving them alone in the large hall.

"You're a fool," Raven said. "I don't need a weapon, you know. I could kill you where you stand with my bare hands."

"I'm sure you could," Nero replied, looking her in the eye. "The question is why don't you?"

Raven stared back at him for several seconds, as if weighing her options. Nero knew that if he had miscalculated he would almost certainly have made a fatal mistake. He was a capable fighter, but he knew he was no match for the young girl standing in front of him.

"The truth is I don't know," Raven replied. "Just a couple of months ago I would have terminated you in an instant, no matter the consequences. And yet, today . . . for reasons I don't quite understand, I do not want to."

"And why do you think that is?" Nero asked.

"Perhaps it is because I do not yet understand you, Nero. I tried to kill you and yet you have shown me nothing but charity. It goes against everything I have been taught."

"From what you have told me in the past few weeks, you have been taught that choice is an illusion. Correct?"

"Yes," Raven replied with a nod. "Madame Furan believes

that we are all just slaves to one degree or another. I could carry out someone else's orders, but then I would merely be swapping one master for another. We all must serve and denying that is pointless."

"People who seek to control others have been repeating that mantra for centuries," Nero said with a frown. "It is no more true today than it was then."

"You serve within your organization," Raven replied, studying him carefully. "You have your masters. How is that any different?"

"The difference is that I serve G.L.O.V.E. by choice," Nero replied. "The reason I'm part of that organization is that I fundamentally believe in freedom. The freedom to act as we choose, to make our own decisions, our own laws. The life of a villain is a life where one must make one's own rules, but still there must be a sense of responsibility. Without that there is nothing but anarchy, chaos, and death. That is what I have always tried to teach the students of this school."

"And yet I remain a prisoner," Raven said.

"You have been kept under guard in order to ensure that you do not endanger the lives of my students and teaching staff, but you are not a prisoner," Nero replied, shaking his head. "If you wish, you may leave now. That is your choice and you will have to live with the consequences. I would very much like you to stay and help me find the Furans so that I can stop them once and for all. The truth is there are some people within G.L.O.V.E. who would have me extract their location from you by force, but that is not my preferred option. I would far rather that you *chose* to help me. If you do choose to leave I will probably be punished for letting you go, but that, in turn, is my decision to make. So what will it be, Raven?"

She stared at him for a moment and he thought he could almost see the battle being fought behind her eyes. She looked down at the floor and then back up at him with just the faintest hint of a smile.

"My name . . . is Natalya."

chapter two

now

Otto stared down at the lights of the city spread out below him and ran his fingers through his snow-white hair. Taking a deep breath he stepped up to the rail that ran around the perimeter of the roof and leaned out over the edge.

"Hard to believe that it was only ten minutes ago that this actually seemed like a good idea," Otto said, staring at the tiny cars passing by on the street hundreds of yards below him.

I would like it noted that I have never classified what you are about to do as a "good idea," a calm voice with a slight synthetic edge said inside Otto's head.

"Yeah, well, you're along for the ride too," Otto said. It had been several months since H.I.V.E.mind, the artificial intelligence that was normally responsible for the day-to-day running of the Higher Institute of Villainous Education had been reinstalled in the tiny organic supercomputer embedded in Otto's skull and by now he had become oddly used to his constant computerized companion. Otto pulled a few feet of wire from the small reel mounted in the middle of his back and secured the end to the steel railing. He pulled the black cowl of the suit of segmented body armor up and over his face. The suit's head-up display flared into life and presented an array of digital readouts at the periphery of his field of vision, each of the suit's systems reporting their own state of readiness. The ISIS, the Integrated Systems Infiltration Suit, was the most sophisticated combat armor in the world and the exclusive property of G.L.O.V.E. It contained technology that every special-ops team on the planet would give anything to get their hands on, but, unlike Otto, they didn't have the right friends in low places.

"Okay," Otto said, "let's get this show on the road."

He tapped a series of commands into the control panel mounted on his forearm and then climbed carefully over the rail, keeping a firm hold as he concentrated on the horizon, trying to ignore the altitude reading on his HUD. Instead he watched the digital clock on the other side of the display that was slowly counting down toward zero. With five seconds to go Otto engaged the ISIS thermoptic camouflage system and the tiny holographic projectors that covered the suit's skin fired up and Otto was instantly rendered all but invisible to the naked eye, only the faintest shimmer in the air betraying his location. The counter reached zero and Otto took a single deep breath before diving head first off the parapet. For a few heart-stopping seconds he plunged down the side of the building in free fall, just inches from the mirrored glass before the brake in the reel on his back engaged and he felt his descent slow dramatically until he was finally hanging stationary. He pushed himself away from the glass and flipped himself over so he was hanging upright before engaging his HUD's thermal imaging system. The mirrored glass faded away to be replaced by a multicolored image of the room inside, where several long banks of boxy objects were glowing with heat. Beyond these objects was another room, within which Otto could see the clear outlines of two people sitting at a desk.

"I've got two guards in the adjoining room," Otto whispered into his throat mic.

"Roger that," a woman's voice with a soft Russian accent replied in his earpiece. "Tripping alarm in three, two, one . . . go."

Otto watched as the two figures inside the building leaped to their feet and ran for the door. As soon as they left the room Otto hit a button on the suit's control panel and a small sphere mounted on his chest lit up with a bright green light as the suit's argon cutting laser came online. Otto watched as the sphere swiveled in its mount, steering the beam in a perfect circle. An instant before the circular cut was complete Otto closed his eyes and reached out with his mind for the building's security systems. It was second nature for him now to tap into the system remotely using the organic computer systems in his head and deactivate the motion sensors in the room just before the thick circle of glass fell on to the carpeted floor inside with a soft thud. Otto pushed away from the glass before swinging back and through the narrow hole in the window. He landed in a crouch, carefully scanning the darkened room as he rose to his feet. Satisfied that his entrance had gone unnoticed, for now at least, he turned back to the window and unclipped himself from the descent cable. He reached into one of the pouches on his belt and pulled four small discs from within before placing one in each corner of the floor-to-ceiling window that he had just cut through.

"I'm in," Otto said. "Two minutes to exfil."

"Understood," the woman's voice replied. "I appear to have the security team's undivided attention. Let me know when you're on your way out."

Otto walked quickly across the room, moving between the banks of computer servers and letting the buzz of the data they were processing wash over him. The information he had come for was not there, but he had not really expected it to be. These machines were wired to the outside world and therefore vulnerable. If what he had come for had been stored on one of those machines then none of this would have been necessary. He moved toward the rear of the room, heading for a steel vault door set into the wall. As he approached he disengaged his suit's camouflage system and the security systems controlling the massive door sensed him approaching as he became visible once more. He tried to mentally connect with the security system, but all he could feel was a confusing jumbled buzz of seemingly random data.

"Looks like the same quantum encryption as we found in Dubai," Otto said. "It's definitely Disciple tech. I get the impression that they really don't want us poking around inside their network."

It would appear so, H.I.V.E.mind replied. *Brute force decryption estimate is three thousand and forty years, nine months, two weeks . . .*

"Okay, I get the point," Otto said. "Looks like we're doing this the hard way. Let's hope that they've not noticed that our guest has gone missing yet."

"Prepare for identification scan," a synthesized voice said as he approached. Otto reached into another pouch on his belt and pulled out a small silver ring-shaped object. He pressed a switch on one side of the ring and several beams of bright white light shot out of it before converging in the air above Otto's hand as a three-dimensional shape began to appear. At first it was just an amorphous hovering blob, but then it began to grow sharper, taking on the shape of a man's head. A few seconds later there was an uncannily lifelike image of a frowning man with a bushy black beard hanging in midair. Otto held the disembodied head up to the scanner mounted in the vault door. It had taken Otto weeks to build a holographic projection system which would have a high enough resolution to fool the scanner and now was the moment he would find out if all of his efforts had actually been worthwhile. The beam of the scanner swept over the hovering face and Otto waited for several long seconds, holding his breath.

"Identity confirmed, Victor Raskoff, access granted," the synthesized voice said and the locking systems within the door disengaged with a whirring clunk and the huge door began to slowly swing open.

"See, I told you it would work," Otto said with a grin. "Now let's see if we can find what we came for."

As he stepped into the vault bright white lights in the ceiling lit up. The walls were lined with shelves on which were stacks of money in every conceivable international denomination and neatly stacked piles of gold bullion. Otto had not gone through all of this to steal anything as mundane as money; what he was there for was far more valuable. He walked to the rear of the room and approached a small steel case on one of the shelves, opened it, and smiled. Inside was a rectangular piece of jet-black glass.

"Bingo," Otto said. "We have a winner, ladies and gentlemen."

He closed the case and lifted it from the shelf, wincing as he heard a soft click from underneath the case and an instant later felt a burst of encrypted data fire through the vault's security system, triggered by the pressure switch that he had just inadvertently released. There was nothing he could do to stop the signal as it set off a building-wide alert. Otto cursed under his breath, taking the black glass object out of its case and slipping it into one of his belt pouches before running back out of the vault.

"Looks like Raskoff left out one tiny little detail of the security system," Otto said into his throat mic. "I think I've probably just set off every alarm in the building."

"Understood," the woman's voice replied in his ear. "I'm on my way out. See you at ground level."

"Roger that," Otto said. "I'm . . ."

His voice was drowned out by the roar of automatic gunfire as several uniformed security guards burst in through the door on the far side of the room and opened fire. Otto sprinted across the room, the servers behind him exploding in a shower of shattered metal and plastic as they were shredded by the hail of bullets. One of the guard's rounds found its target, hitting Otto between the shoulder blades, winding him and knocking him off his feet. He slammed into the ground with a crunch amid the smoldering remnants of the ruined server units.

"Ballistic damage sustained, ISIS systems compromised," a soft synthetic voice said in Otto's ear, as he struggled to catch his breath. "Thermoptic camouflage system offline, ablative armor damage sustained, negative ballistic penetration. System reboot in progress."

Otto winced as he pushed himself up onto his knees. The suit had stopped the bullet, but there was no telling how badly damaged it was without running a full diagnostic. He glanced at the display on his forearm and saw that the reboot of the suit's systems was going to take at least another twenty seconds. Ducking for cover as more gunfire tore into the wall behind him as the security guards advanced toward him, Otto knew he didn't have twenty seconds. He had to get out of there now.

Otto's mind raced, complex calculations balancing time and velocity dancing through his head as he unclipped a cylindrical object from his combat harness. He glanced at the reboot countdown one last time and then tossed the flashbang grenade toward the approaching guards, leaping to his feet as it detonated with a blinding white light and deafening thunderclap. Otto ran toward the window, taking advantage of the guards' momentary disorientation and reached out with his mind for the four tiny explosive charges that he had placed on the window a few minutes earlier. With a tiny mental nudge he triggered their detonators, shattering the window just before he hit it. He dived through the shower of glass and felt his stomach lurch as he launched himself into the void, seeming to hang in the air for an instant before plummeting toward the street far below. Otto watched as the blackened asphalt of the street raced toward him at terminal velocity. He closed his eyes a split second before impact.

He was just five yards from the ground when the ISIS suit rebooted, its variable geometry forcefield generators firing with a soft thumping sound, instantly slowing his descent and reducing Otto's impact with the ground from undoubtedly fatal to merely painful. He hit the street with a crunching thud and lay there winded for a moment before picking himself up from the ground with a pained groan and staggering to his feet. He reached into the pouch on his belt, hoping that the object he had stolen just a minute earlier was still intact. If it had been damaged by his impact with the ground then all of this would have been for nothing. He gingerly pulled the rectangle of black glass from his belt pouch and examined it. Mercifully it still appeared to be in one piece.

"Are you okay?" a voice behind Otto asked. "That looked like a pretty rough landing."

"Yeah," Otto said as Raven approached. "We have to get to the car—we've only got a couple of minutes before they figure out what we've taken and shift their quantum encryption key."

Raven gave a quick nod and they both ran toward a multistory parking structure. Otto glanced over his shoulder as he heard raised voices behind them. On the other side of the street, security guards were pouring from the building that he had left in such dramatic fashion. One of the guards spotted Otto and Raven running into the parking structure and yelled to the others, pointing across the street. Otto and Raven ran past the exit barrier, heading toward the sleek black sports car that was parked just inside the entrance. Otto ran around to the passenger side as Raven climbed into the driver's seat and hit the ignition button in the center of the dashboard. The car sprang to life with a throaty roar and Raven floored the accelerator, sending the low-slung machine rocketing straight through the flimsy wooden barrier and out onto the street beyond. She spun the steering wheel and sent the car into a power slide as the security guards who were sprinting toward them opened fire. The bullets didn't even dent the shining skin of the car, much less penetrate it. Raven accelerated hard and the car surged forward, weaving through the traffic ahead of them as Otto opened the glove compartment in front of him and pulled out a jet-black tablet device. He pushed the black glass rectangle into a slot in the base of the tablet and its screen flared into life, displaying a logo that looked like a stylized image of a circle of barbed wire with a progress bar that was slowly filling beneath it.

"Come on," Otto said impatiently as the sound of sirens started to come from somewhere behind them. As the progress bar slowly filled he could feel only the same incomprehensible buzz of encrypted data coming from the tablet that he had sensed around the vault door a few minutes earlier. The progress bar finally vanished and the barbed-wire logo disappeared to be replaced by a screen displaying an image of a stern-faced man with gray hair and cold blue eyes wearing a dark blue suit with a Stars and Stripes pin in his lapel. Otto's eyes flicked to the name beneath the photo and an instant later the screen went black and the tablet began to emit a high-pitched whine. Without hesitation Otto stabbed at the button to lower the car's window and flung the tablet out through the gap. A split second later there was a flash and the concussive thump of high explosives detonating as the tablet destroyed itself in a ball of fire that would have torn their vehicle to shreds.

"Did you get it?" Raven snapped. "Do we have a name?"

"Yeah, but I'm afraid that things may have just become slightly more complicated," Otto replied.

The screaming sirens of the police cars pursuing them were now getting louder as more patrol cars joined the chase from side streets behind them. Raven frowned at the sight of a road block forming a few hundred yards ahead of them.

"Complicated we can handle, but for now it's time we disappeared," she said, hitting a button on the steering wheel.

The driver in the lead police car gasped in amazement as the black sports car in front of them seemed to flicker for a moment and then vanished, as if it had never been there at all.

☻☻☻

"Hey, guys," Shelby said, flopping down in the seat next to Wing and Franz in Dr. Nero's office.

The three of them were now all that remained of their year's Alpha stream students after the Disciples' merciless assault on the H.I.V.E. training exercise known as the Hunt just a couple of months earlier.

"Good morning," Wing said with a smile. "I missed you at breakfast. Where were you?"

"Worried I might be seeing somebody else, big guy?" Shelby asked with a wink.

"No. Should I be?" Wing asked with a raised eyebrow.

"'Course not," Shelby said with a grin. "Who could ever match you, hot lips?"

"Shelby, I have asked you repeatedly not to call me—"

"How about the smooch-meister then?" Shelby replied quickly. "I actually think I might prefer that to be honest."

"This is being too much information," Franz said under his breath, rolling his eyes.

"If you must know where I was this morning," Shelby said, "Professor Pike never misses breakfast and I was just taking advantage of that fact to . . . erm . . . visit his office." She produced a sheet of folded paper from the pocket of her black uniform jumpsuit. "I know his memory's probably not that great these days, but he really shouldn't just write his master server access passwords down like that."

"And he just left that lying around, did he?" Wing asked with a slight frown.

"Yeah, just lying around . . . in his safe," Shelby said with a mischievous smile, "but if you're going to rely on such basic security you're really asking for this kind of thing to happen."

"I am thinking this is how we usually are starting the whole getting into unbelievably serious trouble thing," Franz said with a resigned sigh. "Normally I am enjoying the whole shooting and exploding and nearly dying thing as much as anyone, but I am wondering perhaps if there is any chance that I might be being allowed to sit this one out for once?"

"No way," Shelby said. "We're like the three musketeers now. *All for one and—*"

"Yes, yes," Franz said, "I was afraid you were going to be saying something like that."

The fact of the matter was that the three of them had become almost inseparable after they became the only remaining Alphas in their year. It had not been easy coping with the loss of their closest friends and the suspicious gossiping whispers of their fellow students that inevitably followed. Nobody would have dared say anything to them directly, but they had become all too used to hushed conversations that stopped as they approached and curious glances in their direction. Everyone else avoided them, as if they were just a lingering reminder of the tragedy that had befallen the school. None of their fellow students seemed to think about the loss that the three of them had suffered as well. They rarely spoke of it, but the death or capture of their fellow Alphas by the Disciples and then the sickening realization that it was all due to the fact that Laura, one of their closest friends, had betrayed them, had been a shattering blow. There were many consequences of that betrayal, including the perhaps fatal shooting of Nigel Darkdoom and Otto's subsequent expulsion from H.I.V.E.

"Dare I ask what exactly you're planning to do with the password?" Wing asked.

"It's a surprise. Tell you later," Shelby whispered as the door hissed open and Dr. Nero walked into the room.

"Good morning," Nero said, sitting down behind his desk. He placed his hand on a panel on the desktop and a millimeter thick tablet slid out from a concealed slot. He tapped at the surface of the tablet and studied the screen for a few seconds. "I see that you have all completed the assignment that I gave you at the end of our last tutorial. Good—now we can move on to the more advanced types of corporate manipulation and examine the use of political donation as effective leverage."

Nero had taken personal charge of supervising the three remaining Alphas after their return to the school, even though it would probably have been easier to simply fold the three of them back into the next year's Alpha stream. It seemed that he was determined that their training in the villainous arts would not be compromised by all that had happened. On the other hand he might just have wanted to keep an especially close eye on the three of them, given their reputation for attracting the wrong kind of trouble.

Nero proceeded with the Villainy Studies lesson for another hour with the three students opposite taking notes on their own tablets and asking the occasional question.

"Excellent," Nero said, as the tutorial drew to a close. "You all seem to have a good grasp of the use of the multinational corporation as a tool for global villainy. Do you have any other questions?"

"Just one," Wing replied, looking Nero in the eye. "Is there any news of the fate of our fellow students yet?"

"I thought that we had already covered this, Mr. Fanchu," Nero replied. "I understand why you are so keen to know more of our pursuit of Anastasia Furan and the rest of the

Disciples, but it would be at best inappropriate and at worst dangerous for me to discuss the details of ongoing operations. You will just have to trust me when I say that we are doing everything we possibly can to track down the students they abducted and rest assured that when we find them—and we *will* find them—I intend to make sure they pay in full for every single drop of blood that they have spilled. All I need you three to do is have faith in the abilities of our operatives and concentrate on the remainder of your education."

"Yeah, that's exactly what you said last time," Shelby said, "and after everything we went through it seems just as unfair as ever that we're being kept out of the loop. They have our friends and—"

"I suggest you think very carefully about who it is you're talking to, Miss Trinity," Nero said, interrupting her with a sudden cold edge to his voice, "or you shall discover just how *unfair* I can be. I will give you any information that I deem appropriate at a time that I deem appropriate. And that is the end of this discussion. Do I make myself clear?"

For a moment Shelby considered arguing the point further, but there was something in the expression on Nero's face that had made her mouth go slightly dry.

"Yes, sir," she said quietly.

"Good," Nero replied. "Now, for tomorrow's lesson I want you to have read and made notes on the first three chapters of Pavel's *Criminal Organization Structural Theory*, one of the finest villainy management theory books ever written. Dismissed."

Nero turned his attention back to the tablet on his desk as Shelby, Wing, and Franz filed out of his office.

"Well, that was going nearly as well as the last time we were asking what was going on with the Disciples," Franz said with a sigh as they walked down the corridor.

"Oh, I don't know," Shelby replied. "I think we managed to irritate him even more this time. It's not like we're asking for specifics; we just want some idea if they're getting any closer to finding them. I don't think that's too much to ask under the circumstances."

"Perhaps the truth is that there is no progress to report," Wing said. "And that is why the question irritates Nero so much."

"It is times like this that I am missing Otto," Franz said. "He would simply be using his computer brain to steal information from Dr. Nero's computer. Much simpler."

"Yeah," Shelby said. "I wonder what he's doing right now?"

"Oh, you know Otto," Wing said with a slight smile, "I'm sure he's keeping out of trouble."

☣☣☣

"Tell me you're joking," Raven said as she sat down opposite Otto.

"I can think of a lot of words I'd use to describe the situation, but funny isn't one of them," Otto replied.

"We go through all that to get the identity of the local Disciple cell commander and now you're telling me that it's Matt Ronson."

"United States Senator Matt Ronson," replied the floating blue wireframe head of H.I.V.E.mind that was being projected from the silver ring lying on the table.

"*Presidential candidate* Senator Matt Ronson," Otto said, rubbing his temples. "And you know what that means."

"A full Secret Service security detail," Raven replied with a sigh, "and he's the only person who might be able to give us any clue where Furan might be hiding."

"We don't even know that for sure, but the only way we'll find out is if we ask him a few friendly questions," Otto replied. "And unlike the cell leader in London, let's see if we can ask those questions *before* he ends up under a train."

"I thought we weren't going to mention that again," Raven said with a slight frown.

"Just making an observation," Otto said with a crooked smile. "Any idea how on earth we're going to pull this off?"

"I was just about to ask you the same thing," Raven replied, shaking her head.

"Well, he's on the campaign trail at the moment," Otto replied, "which means that the first thing we need to work out is when and where to go after him. Once we've figured that out we can start to think about how we're going to get past his security detail."

"I'm going to have to talk to Nero," Raven said with a sigh. "I'll need to clear it with him before we go after a target this high profile. I think I can already imagine his reaction."

"Better now than later when he might just have won the election," Otto said. "If you think he's going to be a hard man to get to at the moment, just imagine what it would be like trying to reach him once he's comfortably settled in the White House."

"Point taken," Raven replied. "I don't imagine that Nero's going to be pleased at the prospect of a senior member of the Disciples in the Oval Office. We have enough to worry about at the moment as it is, without adding that into the mix."

Otto stared at the silver ring that was projecting the hovering image of H.I.V.E.mind and then at the discarded ISIS armor on the bench nearby. He suddenly felt the familiar prickle of an idea forming.

"I think I may have an idea of how we can get close enough to him to get what we need, but I'll need some components from Professor Pike and some tinkering time," Otto said, staring out of the window.

"Draw up a list and I'll pass it on to Nero when I report

in," Raven replied with a nod. "The sooner we get this done, the better."

⊛⊛⊛

Laura Brand pushed herself up onto her hands and knees, before staggering back to her feet, the sharp metallic taste of blood filling her mouth.

"Too slow," the girl standing opposite her said with a nasty smile, "always too slow."

The girl advanced toward Laura again, her fists raised, forcing her back toward the walls of the pit that surrounded them. She struck like lightning, her foot lashing out and hitting Laura in the ribs, knocking the wind out of her and sending her staggering backward. She felt the cold, hard concrete of the pit wall against her back as the other girl pulled back her fist for a final blow.

"Enough," a voice shouted from somewhere in the darkness behind the bright white floodlights that illuminated the pit. "One two five, you fought well, you may return to your quarters. I shall deal with three seven nine."

The other girl lowered her fist with a nod and walked across the pit toward the steel door set into the opposite wall. She glanced back over her shoulder at Laura, a cruel sneer on her face, as the sound of heavy bolts unlocking came from the other side of the door.

"Typical H.I.V.E. brat," the girl said. "No fight in you."

Laura glared back at the other girl, wiping away the blood that trickled from her lip with the back of her hand. The door swung open and a tall, muscular man with a square jaw and shaved head walked into the room, watching in silence as Laura's opponent left. His name was Heinrich, Furan's right-hand man, and over the recent months he had become a regular feature in Laura's all too frequent nightmares.

"I still do not understand why Furan tolerates your weakness," the man said, looking at Laura with undisguised contempt. "If it were up to me I'd have thrown you to the wolves weeks ago."

Laura did not reply; instead she just stared at the blood-stained concrete floor. She had learned the hard way that no one answered back to this man. Her life at the Glasshouse, Anastasia Furan's training facility for young assassins, had taught her many harsh lessons. Her former life at H.I.V.E. might have been hard at times, but it was nothing compared to the ordeal she had been put through since she had been captured by Furan and thrown into this fresh new hell. Here there was no tolerance for weakness, no pause for rest, and no hope of escape.

"Look at me," Heinrich snapped.

Laura lifted her head and looked into his cold gray eyes.

"Such weakness," he said, "and yet I still see some shred of that defiance you showed when you first arrived here, three seven nine. Most of the other H.I.V.E. students we captured are either dead or have broken by now, but you're still clinging on to something, aren't you? What is it? Tell me."

"Not something . . . someone," Laura replied quietly.

"Really?" Heinrich replied. "And just who might that be?"

"Someone who won't stop until he's found this place and burned it to the ground," Laura said defiantly.

"You're talking about Nero, aren't you?" Heinrich said, stepping toward her. "Do you really think he cares about you, three seven nine? The girl who betrayed him. The girl who is responsible for the death of so many of his students. I think you overestimate your value to him. If he was coming to rescue you or any of the rest of his brats, do you not think he would have done so by now?"

Laura felt a sudden wave of despair as Heinrich reminded her of what she had done. She had been blackmailed into revealing the location of the H.I.V.E. survival training exercise known as the Hunt, unaware that she was jeopardizing the lives of her friends and fellow students. There was barely a waking hour that passed when she was not haunted by that memory and now Heinrich was taking obvious delight in twisting that particular knife.

"He won't be coming for me," Laura replied. "He'll be coming for the others and I hope for your sake you're not here when he does."

"I'm not afraid of Nero," Heinrich said with a twisted

smile. "By the time that Furan's finished with him, he'll *wish* he was dead. Nero's time is past. Very soon the world will belong to the Disciples and there's nothing Nero, G.L.O.V.E. or anyone else will be able to do to stop it."

"They've stopped you before, they'll stop you again," Laura said.

Heinrich gave her a swift backhanded blow to the face and Laura gasped in pain.

"Clean yourself up," Heinrich said, "then return to your cell."

He walked out of the pit and Laura followed him into the spartan bathroom beyond. She walked to one of the steel basins attached to the gray concrete walls and turned on the tap, splashing the icy water on her face, watching as the trail of blood washed away down the drain. She pulled a couple of rough paper towels from the dispenser on the wall and carefully dried her aching face. She stared for a moment at her reflection in the mirror screwed onto the wall. The fresh cuts and bruises on her face were starting to feel normal after the months she had spent being subjected to the worst the Glasshouse had to offer. The bloodstains on the white vest she wore would have to stay there for now. They got a clean uniform once a week, a clean vest and a pair of gray camouflage combat pants to go with the regulation black leather boots. You trained in that uniform, you ate in that uniform, and you slept in that uniform. That was the way the Glasshouse worked. She let out a sigh and walked out of the bathroom and into the corridor that led back to her cell. She came out on to the balcony that ran around the huge circular central atrium of the underground facility. The center of the atrium was dominated by the inverted steel and glass spire that hung from the ceiling and which housed the facility's control center. Wasp-like camera drones with whirring cowled rotors flew around the atrium, tracking the facility's trainees' movements using the barcodes printed on the back of their vests. There was rarely such a thing as privacy here. Laura looked over the balcony and down to the ground far below where trainees were receiving a hand-to-hand combat lesson in the large open training area.

The lowest levels housed the dormitories, but Laura was not afforded the comparative luxury of sharing a living space with the other trainees. She was kept in one of the isolation cells on the upper levels and that was where she was heading right now. At first she had wondered why Furan had singled her out for such treatment, but eventually she had decided that it was all part of the perverse delight that the woman took in tormenting her. She made her way to her cell on the other side of the atrium and the door unlocked with a clunk. She pushed it open and stepped inside, closing it behind her. The door locked again and she sat down on the concrete block with a thin mattress on top that was the Glasshouse's version of a bed. The only other things in the room were a stainless-steel sink and toilet. Laura lay back on the mattress and closed her eyes. She refused to give in to despair, no matter how tempting it was at times. Instead, she thought of her friends and her previous life at H.I.V.E. and silently prayed that she might one day return there and see them again.

chapter three

The black limousine rounded the corner of the hangar and slowed to a halt at the bottom of the steps that led up into the sleek fuselage of the private jet standing on the tarmac. A Secret Service agent stepped out of the car and opened the rear door. Senator Matt Ronson climbed out of the car and trotted up the steps leading into the plane. With his swept-back silver hair, immaculate suit, and healthy tan, he was the very image of the successful American businessman and there was no bigger business than his current occupation. What neither the people who had elected him nor the men who had selected him as their party's presidential candidate knew was that he was one of the most senior members of the organization known as the Disciples. That organization had been highly effective in ensuring his rapid rise through the political ranks and now he stood on the brink of claiming the most powerful office in the world. He smiled contentedly to himself as he sat down in one of the large leather seats that lined the cabin. His latest poll figures were excellent and all of the projections appeared to indicate that he would soon be moving into a new house on Pennsylvania Avenue. It didn't hurt that one of the Disciples' front companies was responsible for manufacturing the electronic voting machines that would be used in some of the most closely contested states during the upcoming election. Even if the electorate were foolish enough to choose his opponent the final result would be no different. All he had to do was sit and wait for November.

"Your wife and son will be here shortly, Senator," the Secret Service agent reported. "They were slightly late leaving the hotel, but the pilot assures me that we can make up the time once we get airborne."

"Good," Ronson replied. "I have a meeting that I can't be late for." The meeting in question was a teleconference with the other members of the Disciples and he was keen to get an update on how Anastasia Furan's plan was developing. Nero and G.L.O.V.E. had been a thorn in their sides for far too long and it was about time they were finished off once and for all. Furan had dealt Nero a stunning blow with the assault on the H.I.V.E. training exercise known as the Hunt and now was the time to press home their advantage. Nero's status with the other members of the global fraternity of villains had been weakened by his failure to protect his students and it would not take much to amplify that chaos still further. If Nero finally lost his grip on the reins of power, his fellow villains would turn on him in an instant, that much was certain. Ronson's cell phone started ringing and he glanced at the screen to see that his campaign manager was calling. He took the call just as his wife and son climbed aboard and the jet's engines began to spin up. He mouthed "You're late" to his wife as she sat down across the aisle from him and she mouthed a "Sorry" in reply as the plane taxied for takeoff. He spent ten minutes discussing the latest polling data with his campaign director before finally hanging up.

"What kept you?" Ronson asked his wife with a frown.

"Sorry," she replied. "I had to get changed."

Ronson's frown deepened. There was something funny about his wife's voice. Her usual midwest twang was gone, replaced instead by what sounded like a soft Russian accent.

"We both did," his son added, in a British accent.

Ronson's eyes widened in shock as their faces shimmered and faded to reveal a pair of smooth black skintight masks, with mirrored silver eyepieces. The pair of impostors pulled off the masks, revealing two faces that Ronson found horrifyingly familiar.

"Good morning, Senator Ronson," Otto said with a smile as Raven pulled a snub-nosed pistol from her handbag and leveled it at him. "I do hope we're not interrupting anything."

"What have you done with my wife and son?" Ronson demanded, slowly sliding his hand into his pocket.

"Oh, they're fine," Otto replied, "if a little unconscious at the moment. As are the two Secret Service agents in the rear compartment that you just tried to summon with the panic button in your pocket. I took the liberty of disabling it the moment I boarded the plane anyway, just in case. We wouldn't want any air force jets interrupting our little chat now, would we?"

"Don't bother shouting for the pilots either," Raven said calmly. "They are equally . . . indisposed. Now, hands where I can see them." Ronson complied, lifting his hands in front of him defensively.

"Then who's flying the plane?" Ronson asked, a slight note of panic in his voice.

"I am," Otto said, glancing toward the cockpit. "You've got to love fly-by-wire avionics."

"You won't get away with this," Ronson said.

"You'd be surprised how often I hear that," Otto replied with a sly smile. "Now, let's cut to the chase, shall we? I'm sure you know who we both are since you're a senior member of the Disciples, so I'm equally sure that you're aware that my friend here is really unbelievably good at hurting people. All we want to know is where Furan is and where she's keeping the H.I.V.E. students she captured. If you tell us with a minimum of fuss there'll be no need for them to hose down the interior of this plane after we land, if you catch my drift."

Ronson glanced at Raven. They had all heard the horror stories that were told about her among the massed ranks of global villainy. The way she was looking at him gave him no reason to doubt that those stories were true.

"I don't know where the Glasshouse is," Ronson replied, shaking his head. "No one does."

Otto noticed Raven's eyes widen very slightly. He knew by now that was about as close as she normally came to being shocked by anything.

"The Glasshouse is gone," Raven said, a dangerous edge to her voice. "I watched it burn."

"The original Glasshouse, yes," Ronson said, "but she had a new facility built in a hidden location. No one knows where it is except Furan and a handful of her most trusted people. She has not shared its location with any of the rest of us."

"And you expect me to believe that?" Raven asked, lowering her pistol and pointing it at Ronson's knee. "I read that you enjoy running to keep fit. Such a shame." She cocked the hammer.

"Wait, please," Ronson begged. "I swear it's the truth. Furan's paranoid about security—we don't even know what country the Glasshouse is in, let alone its precise location."

His pupil dilation and cardio-pulmonary activity indicate an honest response, H.I.V.E.mind said inside Otto's head.

"I think our friend here might be telling the truth," Otto said.

"I agree," Raven said, "and unfortunately for you that means that you're no use to us," Raven said, leveling the pistol at his forehead.

"Wait, wait," Ronson said frantically. "There is one person who might know where Furan is."

"Talk," Raven replied.

"The only person who might be able to tell you is the man who designed the facility," Ronson said quickly. "Furan let it slip that her new facility had been designed by the Architect."

"The Architect is a myth," Raven said, shaking her head slightly.

"No, he's real, I swear," Ronson said, sweat beading on his forehead. "He's the only person who Furan would have trusted to have designed it. Think about it—who else could she be sure would never talk?"

"Supposing I believe you," Raven said with a frown, "and the Architect did build a new Glasshouse for Furan? Where would I find him?"

"I have no idea," Ronson replied. "You've heard the same rumors I have, no doubt. You don't find the Architect unless he wants you to find him. I've never met anyone who has ever seen the man, much less talked to him."

Raven stared at Ronson for a few seconds and then reached into her handbag and produced a pair of handcuffs.

"Cuff yourself to the seat," Raven said. "I need to have a private conversation with my associate and I don't want you going anywhere."

Raven watched as Ronson did as he was instructed. She checked that he was firmly shackled to his seat before she gestured with a nod for Otto to join her in the plane's rear compartment. He followed her into the conspicuously less comfortable area that provided seating for Ronson's staff, who in this case were the two unconscious Secret Service agents slumped in their seats.

"Find us somewhere to land," Raven said. "If what he's telling us is true, then we have a considerably more difficult job ahead of us than we had anticipated."

"I'll try to find somewhere quiet," Otto said, "but it's going to start alarm bells ringing when a plane carrying a passenger like this diverges from its flight plan."

"We'll be long gone by the time the authorities arrive," Raven replied. "Good work on the masks by the way."

Otto had spent the previous couple of days adapting the hoods from the ISIS suits and combining them with the new holographic projector he had designed in such a way that their optical camouflage hologram projectors would display a perfect copy of any face that they scanned in. It had been relatively straightforward from a technical point of view. The hard part had been obtaining the high-resolution scans of Ronson's wife and son's heads. He'd left that part of the plan to Raven.

"It was just a small logical step from what the suit masks already did really," Otto said. "It was no big deal."

I have found a suitable landing site, H.I.V.E.mind said. *It is an abandoned military airstrip that is only a few miles from our current flight path. It should serve our purposes.*

"Okay," Otto said, "H.I.V.E.mind's found us somewhere to put this thing on the ground."

"Good. I'll go and take care of Ronson," Raven said, gesturing toward the forward compartment with her pistol.

"No," Otto said. "I've got a better idea."

"Nero made it quite clear that he was to be taken out of play," Raven said. "We can't take the chance that he'll end up as president."

"I know," Otto replied. "Trust me."

Fifteen minutes later the jet touched down on the crumbling tarmac of the disused military runway. As soon as the plane stopped moving, the hatch popped open and Raven dragged the unconscious bodies of the Secret Service agents and the two pilots out onto the dusty scrubland next to the runway.

"Make it quick," Raven said to Otto as she headed through the exit hatch for the final time.

Otto gave a quick nod and headed back into the forward compartment, where Ronson sat slumped, still shackled to his seat.

"Please," Ronson begged, "I can help you. I have more information I can give you, just don't let her kill me."

"Don't worry, she's not going to kill you," Otto said. "I am."

Otto closed his eyes for a moment and reached out with his senses for the jet's autopilot system.

"The Disciples abducted and imprisoned some of my best friends and murdered dozens of my classmates," Otto said, fixing Ronson with an icy stare. "Did you really think there wasn't going to be a price to pay for that?"

The jet's engines began to spin up as Otto turned his back on Ronson and headed out of the forward cabin. He climbed out of the hatch and down the stairs to the tarmac. As he walked away from the plane, he connected to the plane's controls and the hatch whirred shut behind him. The plane began to turn in a tight circle, leaving it pointing back down the runway.

"*Bon voyage*," Otto said, closing his eyes and mentally activating the autopilot. The plane's twin engines throttled up and it accelerated away down the wide strip of tarmac, before lifting off and banking away into the bright blue sky.

"It should run out of fuel somewhere over the Atlantic,"

Otto said, his voice calm. "Plenty of time for him to think about it."

"A bullet would have been quicker," Raven said, watching the departing jet as it grew smaller and smaller.

"Too quick," Otto said. "Let's get out of here."

⊛ ⊛ ⊛

Laura placed the metal tray on the tabletop and sat down on the bench. The sectioned compartments of the tray contained portions of brown and gray sludge and a couple of dry military-ration biscuits. It was the only meal that the Glasshouse trainees ever ate and while it might mean they didn't starve it was a very long way from appetizing. Another tray clanked down on to the table and she looked up to see Nigel Darkdoom taking a seat opposite her.

"You okay?" Nigel whispered. Chatter was frowned upon during mealtimes and though the guards on the far side of the room seemed not to care there was no point giving them a reason to start swinging their stun batons. Nigel frowned as he saw the fresh cuts and bruises on Laura's face.

"Yeah, I'm fine," Laura replied with a sigh. "Just took another beating in the pit. It's nothing. How are you feeling?"

Nigel had taken several months to fully recover from the gunshot wound he had suffered when the Disciples ambushed the Hunt. In truth, he had been lucky to survive but he still looked thin and he tired quickly.

"Better every day," Nigel said. "The doctor said that I should be ready to start with physical training in a couple of weeks. Though looking at you I'm not sure that's actually a good thing."

"Yeah, well no one hates you the way they do me," Laura said, glancing across the room at the table where the other captured H.I.V.E. Alpha stream students all sat together, eating in silence. Within just a couple of hours of arriving at the Glasshouse, Furan had gathered them together to explain the situation they now found themselves in. She had made it clear that escape was impossible and that any attempt to prove otherwise had only one punishment: immediate summary execution. Just when Laura had thought that things could not get any bleaker Furan had then, with obvious pleasure, explained to the other H.I.V.E. students that the reason they were in such danger was because of Laura's treachery. She had neglected to mention that the only reason Laura had betrayed the school was in a desperate attempt to save the lives of her parents and newborn baby brother, who were being held hostage by the Disciples. From that point, her life had been a living hell; on one side were the existing Glasshouse trainees, who hated all of the captured H.I.V.E. students, and on the other were her former classmates, who now blamed her for not only their capture but also the deaths of many of their friends. The only people who still spoke to her were Nigel, Tom, and Penny, all of whom had been present when Laura's betrayal had first been exposed. They were the only ones who understood the nightmarish position that Laura had been put in and even they had still found it hard to forgive her. She knew how they felt; she still had not forgiven herself.

"I've tried to explain what happened to people," Nigel said quietly, "but most of them don't want to hear it. It's going to take time."

"Oh, I don't expect anyone to forgive me," Laura said, pushing the gray slop on her tray around with her plastic spoon. "Even you, Nigel."

"Yeah, well, that's not your call," Nigel said with a tiny smile. "I don't care what anyone else thinks. I know you, Laura, and I know that you'd never have given them the information they wanted if you'd known what the consequences would be. We've got to try and stay positive if we're going to have any hope of surviving this place."

Tom and Penny walked past Laura and Nigel and sat down opposite each other at the far end of the table. The last traces of Penny's exuberantly pink hair had vanished weeks ago, to be replaced by her natural shade of dark brown and she too bore the marks of the Glasshouse's training—a fresh pink scar on her neck from a recent defeat in a "mock" knife fight. Tom glanced over at Laura and gave a small nod as their eyes met. The pair of them had barely spoken to Laura since they had arrived at the Glasshouse, partly because they did not want to incur the wrath of the other captured H.I.V.E. students, but also, Laura suspected, because they too blamed her for their current predicament.

"I understand that, Nigel," Laura replied, a sudden look of deep sadness in her eyes, "but what if there's no one coming for us? What if they can't find us? What if they don't want to?"

"You can't think like that," Nigel said, shaking his head. "You know they won't give up on us, Nero, my father, Otto, and the others, so we mustn't give up on them." He paused, glancing at the guard who was wandering across the room toward them. "That witch Furan wants nothing more than to break us and so we mustn't lose faith, because if we do, she wins."

☻ ☻ ☻

"This is an . . . unexpected development," Nero said with a slight frown. Across from him, on the opposite side of H.I.V.E.'s main conference room table, sat the semi-transparent holographic projections of Raven and Otto. "I was pleased to hear that Senator Ronson had met with such an unfortunate *accident*, but assuming that what he told us

60

was true, and we have no reason to suspect otherwise, we may now only have one remaining clue as to the whereabouts of Furan and our students."

"The Architect," Otto said.

"Exactly," Nero replied.

"Is he even real?" Raven asked. "I mean, I've heard the stories, just like everyone else, but I always thought they were just that . . . stories."

"Oh, I can assure you he is quite real," Nero said with a sigh. "Indeed, we have a certain amount of, shall we say, *history*."

"So just who is he?" Otto asked. "And why is he so important?"

"As you are well aware, Mr. Malpense, there are times when members of our fraternity find themselves in need of elaborate but well-hidden facilities."

"Every good villain should have a secret base," Otto replied, with a slight smile.

"Precisely," Nero said with a nod, "but it is phenomenally difficult to construct that kind of project in total secrecy. Quite aside from discreetly obtaining extremely large quantities of construction materials, one must also recruit a skilled workforce that can work quickly and efficiently in often extremely hostile environments and can also be relied upon to keep the nature of that work absolutely secret."

"So say, for example, you wanted a school built inside an

active volcano and didn't want anyone finding out about it, he's the man to call."

"Yes, though he was actually only partially responsible for the design of this facility," Nero replied. "Which is also part of the reason I've not had any contact with him in recent years."

"And now he's working for the Disciples," Raven said.

"Oh, he doesn't work *for* anyone," Nero replied, "he works for whoever has the most interesting project to offer him. He is not the sort of man who would trouble himself worrying about which side he was working for. That neutrality is part of the reason that he has managed to survive in our murderous little world for as long as he has."

"So he's not a Disciple, but he's not part of G.L.O.V.E. either," Otto said. "So why would he help us?"

"I'm not sure he will," Nero said with a sigh. "In fact, I rather suspect that he won't. Especially if you mention my involvement."

"So where do we go from here?" Otto asked.

"If I had his location, perhaps I could *persuade* him to tell us where to find Furan," Raven said.

"Thank you, Natalya," Nero said, shaking his head, "but I'd rather it didn't come to that. He may not want to meet me, but there is someone that he would talk to. Get ready to move. I'll contact you later."

He cut off the connection and Otto and Raven's

holographic projections flickered and vanished. Nero stared into space for a moment, lost in thought, before tapping a command into the touch screen embedded in the surface of the table in front of him. A few seconds later, another glowing figure coalesced out of thin air on the other side of the table.

"Hello, Max," the tall, bald man said, "what can I do for you?"

"Hello, Diabolus," Nero said with a smile. "I have a favor to ask. I need you to talk to an old friend."

☢ ☢ ☢

Anastasia Furan felt a cold fury building inside her as she read the report on the mysterious aviation accident that had claimed the life of Senator Matt Ronson. She had been instrumental in steering his rise through the political ranks and now all of that appeared to have been wasted effort. While it would not have been the first time that a member of their shadowy world had occupied the White House, it would have been extremely useful for her future plans if she had been able to dictate the response of the United States government once those plans went into full effect.

"How did this happen?" Furan said angrily. Her entire head was covered in horrific twisted burn scars, such that there was no longer any trace of her once great beauty. She wore gloves, a long black coat, and a high-necked black blouse that covered every other square inch of her skin.

"We're not sure," the nervous-looking man standing on the other side of her desk said. "Our sources within the American intelligence services have told us that they are just as puzzled about what happened. Somebody took out Ronson's security detail and the two pilots and then it appears that they crashed the plane into the ocean with the senator still on board. They found floating debris from the crash this morning, but they're still searching for the plane's flight recorder. They should know more when they find it. Whoever did this, it was a suicide mission, so they're working on the assumption that it was an act of terrorism at this point."

"You're assuming that whoever was responsible was on board when it crashed," Furan replied. "And why did the Secret Service logs show Ronson's wife and child as having left the hotel for the airport and yet they were later found unconscious in their room."

"As I say," the man replied, "there are many unanswered questions."

"First our cell leader in London is pushed in front of a train and then someone steals a data slab from our field office in Chicago. Raskoff may have insisted that there was no sensitive data on the device that was stolen, but I fear it may be more than a coincidence that within a week our

American cell commander is dead too. It looks to me like someone has declared open season on senior members of our organization and I think I know exactly who that is."

"Nero," the man replied.

"Yes," Furan said with a nod. "I expected reprisals after we attacked his beloved students, of course, but I did not think they would be this effective or brutal. I knew he would send Natalya after us, but there's more to it than that. I want our best men on this. I want to know how they got to Ronson and I want to know where they intend to hit us next. Project Absalom is at too critical a stage for us to be distracted by this now. Increase the security details on our senior commanders and brief them fully on the threat. Make sure that any sighting of Raven is reported immediately. She will not catch us out so easily again."

"Understood," the man replied with a nod and walked out of her office.

Furan stood up from her desk and walked over to the far wall where a portrait of her late brother, Pietor Furan, hung. She stared at the picture for a few seconds before reaching out and laying a hand on the canvas.

"Soon, Pietor," she said softly, "soon you will be avenged."

☻☻☻

The young man ran across the crowded office, carrying a single sheet of paper. He stopped at an office door on the other side of the room that bore the words "Robert Flack, Director of Operations, Artemis Section." He knocked once on the door and a few seconds later a voice shouted for him to come in.

"What can I do for you, Mr. Simons?" Flack asked as the young analyst walked into his office.

"I thought you'd want to see this, sir," Simons said, placing the sheet of paper on the desk in front of him. Printed on it was a black-and-white image that, judging by the poor quality, had been captured from a surveillance-camera feed. It showed a fuzzy image of a teenage boy and a tall dark-haired woman walking through a pair of large glass doors. The only thing unusual about the boy was the spiky snow-white hair on his head.

"Shut the door," Flack said, studying the image. "When and where was this taken?"

"Yesterday morning," Simons replied, "at the Ritz Carlton in Phoenix. The Secret Service had been running all of the surveillance feed to see if they could identify whoever it was that attacked Senator Ronson's wife and son. Our facial-recognition software raised a possible Person of Interest flag and when I checked the alert it was level five."

Level five was the highest-level flag that could be assigned to an individual by Artemis Section. The section was one of the most secretive and powerful branches of the Central Intelligence Agency. Their job was simple: They found people, people who almost invariably wanted very much not to be found, and they were exceptionally good at their job. As head of the section Robert Flack joked that he reported to only two people, God and the President, and that unlike the President he was an atheist. Now he studied the photo, peering over the half-moon glasses that were perched on the end of his nose. A frown appeared on his gaunt, almost skeletal face as he turned his attention to the woman walking beside the boy in the photo.

"That's definitely Malpense," Flack said, gesturing for Simons to take the seat on the other side of the desk, "but who's this with him, I wonder."

It had been over six months since Flack had been personally instructed by the President with discovering all there was to know about the mysterious young man known as Otto Malpense. They had first become aware of Malpense when he had saved the President's life when Airforce One had been hijacked in midair by terrorists. He had then been taken into custody by the disgraced rogue intelligence agency H.O.P.E. and subsequently vanished. Several months after that he had contacted the President during the crisis that had arisen when hostile forces had attacked the Army's Advanced Weapons Project facility and taken various high-ranking military officers and civilians hostage. The boy had persuaded the President to give him the launch codes to Thor's Hammer, an orbital nuclear-weapon launch platform, and had then used it to destroy a weaponized nanite swarm that would otherwise have almost certainly killed every living thing on the face of the planet. Immediately after this incident, the truth of which was only known to a handful people outside of the Oval Office, the President had ordered Flack to find out just who Otto Malpense was and whether he posed an ongoing threat to the nation's security. The stark fact of the matter was that Flack knew almost as little about Otto Malpense today as he had when he had been tasked with the investigation. He had been a prisoner of H.O.P.E. for some considerable time, but all of that agency's records had been lost during the chaos of its dramatic collapse. As it stood he had little more than the boy's name and a handful of images. Now here he was, walking into the same hotel that Matt Ronson had been staying at on the night before he died in such mysterious circumstances.

"She's no one," Simons replied, "apparently."

"Really?" Flack said, sounding surprised. "You ran her?"

"Through every database we have," Simons replied. "Not one hit. She's a ghost."

"There's no such thing, Simons, you know that."

"I know, sir, but there's no trace of an ID for her."

Flack's puzzled frown deepened further. By this point in the twenty-first century it was staggeringly difficult to erase all traces of a person's identity. The American government alone had poured trillions of dollars into making sure that they could always put a name to a face. Beating the system and moving around freely on American soil was supposed to be next to impossible.

"Do you want me to broaden the search?" Simons asked. "I could put this out on the black net and see who bites."

"No," Flack said. "The last thing I want is to spook Malpense and whoever this woman is and send them into hiding. I'm going to feed her image to some allied agencies and see if we can get any hits in the next few days. If she is with Malpense we can track him that way without flagging our interest in him to anyone else."

"Okay, boss," Simons replied. He was halfway to Flack's office door when he turned back with a half-smile on his face. "I don't suppose you can tell me who this kid is and why everyone's so interested in him, can you?"

"Sure, no problem," Flack said, raising an eyebrow. "All you have to do is get yourself elected President."

chapter four

Wing stood in the doorway of Shelby's room keeping watch for any sign of one of H.I.V.E.'s many security guards while Shelby and Franz sat staring at the monitor attached to the terminal on her desk.

"I am thinking that maybe we are needing Otto or Laura at this point," Franz said with a puzzled frown as he examined the text on the screen.

"Yeah, well, we're just going to have to do our best without them," Shelby replied. "I think I'm nearly there. If I just try and log in through this proxy then—"

Shelby's terminal emitted a loud warning tone and the screen went black save for two lines of glowing red text in the center of the screen.

ACCESS DENIED
ONE LOGIN ATTEMPT REMAINING

"Damn!" Shelby spat, slamming her hand down on the desk. "I was sure that was it."

"I am thinking it is a good thing that H.I.V.E.mind is offline for maintenance," Franz said with a sigh. The artificial intelligence that normally ran the school's electrical and data systems had been down for the past couple of months. There had been no real explanation as to why, other than Professor Pike occasionally muttering something under his breath about "substantial upgrades."

"At least if he was online we could just ask him nicely what's going on," Shelby said, "instead of trying to pretend that I know what I'm doing with one of these things. Who knows what kinds of alarms I'm going to trigger if I keep messing around like this. I should have guessed it wouldn't be easy. I just figured that if we had Pike's login we'd be able to get access, but there are so many extra levels of security. I know that it pays to be careful, but Nero has the network locked down tight. I've no doubt that Snow White or Laura could waltz past it all, but I never really got the hang of this whole hacking thing. Just don't have the nerd gene, I guess."

"You can't blame Nero for being cautious. After the attack on the Hunt he has good reason to be slightly paranoid. I think it's time we found an alternate means of acquiring the information," Wing said.

"I'm open to suggestions at this point," Shelby said with a sigh. "Because I am officially out of ideas."

"I am having one idea," Franz said, "but it is being the long shoot."

"Okay, I'd be willing to try just about anything at this point," Shelby said.

"We will be harnessing the power of mesmerism," Franz said conspiratorially. "If Doctor Nero will not be giving us this information willingly then we will using the power of the mind to compel him to be telling us."

"Erm, Franz," Shelby said, "are you suggesting that we *hypnotize* Nero?"

"Ja," Franz replied, "once he is being in a hypnotic trance he will be telling us everything we want to know. I have been doing some research and I believe I could induce such a trance."

Shelby, for once, looked like she was lost for words, simply staring back at Franz with a look of utter disbelief on her face.

"Franz, correct me if I am wrong," Wing said, "but even if you do believe in the power of hypnotic compulsion, isn't it only supposed to work on the weak-willed?"

"Yes, that is being correct." Franz nodded.

"And so you would classify Doctor Nero, a man who single-handedly controls the massed ranks of global villainy, runs the most secret school on the planet, and faces constant and serious threats to his life from all directions, in fact, altogether one of the most powerful and cunning men on the planet as *weak-willed?*"

"Not to mention the fact that we would presumably also have to persuade him to sit down while the Great Franz, Hypnotist Extraordinaire, dangles a pocket watch in front of his face," Shelby said.

"I am admitting that there may be some small kinks to be ironed out in the plan," Franz said, looking slightly uncomfortable.

"Franz," Shelby said, standing up and grabbing him by both shoulders, "that is perhaps . . . no wait . . . that is quite definitely the worst plan that I have heard since some idiot suggested that we try to escape from H.I.V.E. through the laundry system. Well done."

"There is no need to be being rude about it," Franz said with an indignant sniff. "I am just trying to be helping."

"I need to go for a walk," Shelby said, shaking her head. "Come on, let's get out of here." She strode past Wing and onto the walkway balcony that ran around the outside of the enormous cavern that housed accommodation block seven, their home since their arrival at H.I.V.E.

"Actually," Wing said quietly to Franz, as they walked along a few yards behind Shelby, "I thought it was quite a good plan, it just requires quite a lot of . . . refinement. Perhaps, for now, we just need something a bit more conventional."

"Thank you, Wing," Franz said. "I was knowing that you were being a person of vision, but maybe you are being right. I will be stopping thinking outside the bag."

The three of them headed down the stairs at the end of the walkway and out into the cavern's central atrium. They took no notice of the students who fell silent as they walked past or who eyed them with suspicion from across the room. They were halfway across the huge room when they spotted Professor Pike walking into the accommodation block with a frown on his face. He looked around for a moment and then spotted Shelby, Wing, and Franz and headed toward them.

"Uh-oh," Shelby said quietly. "What does he want?"

"I can make an educated guess," Wing said as the white-haired old man approached.

"Ahhh, Miss Trinity, Mr. Fanchu, Mr. Argentblum," he said, nodding to each of them in turn, "just the people I was looking for. I was wondering if you could help me with something?"

"Of course, Professor," Wing replied calmly. "What can we do for you?"

"I seem to have misplaced a rather important piece of paper," the Professor said with the vaguest hint of a smile. "I don't suppose you've seen it lying around anywhere, have you? I could have sworn I left it in my safe in my office, but I'm getting very absentminded in my old age and if someone did happen upon it I would hate for them to try and use it *incorrectly*."

"We'll . . . erm . . . keep an eye out for it," Shelby replied.

"Good, please do," the Professor said, "because if someone did, for example, make two failed attempts to access the master server and then subsequently make a third attempt that failed, it would cause all sorts of flags to pop up at the central security command station. Which would be most uncomfortable for all concerned. If, however, they were to use it in combination with an access key like this," the Professor reached into the pocket of his lab coat and produced a tiny thumb drive, "they would probably be able to read all kinds of interesting information. The sort of information that some people don't think it would hurt for them to have access to perhaps. The real beauty of it would be that nobody would ever know. Mr. Fanchu, would you mind holding this while I find my glasses?" He gave the access key to Wing and began patting his pockets. "Oh blast, where are they?"

"Professor," Shelby said, pointing at the glasses perched on top of his head.

"Aaaah, of course," the Professor said, pulling the glasses down onto his face. "Thank you, Miss Trinity, like I said, I'm becoming so very absentminded. I'm always forgetting where things are or that I've given them to people. Anyway, must dash, toodle-pip!"

With that he turned back toward the entrance to the accommodation block. He walked a few yards and then stopped.

"By the way, Miss Trinity," he said, "I've scheduled in a few extra cyber-security seminars for you. Something tells me you need them. Not all locks can be picked physically, you know."

Shelby, Wing, and Franz watched as he walked away and then all three of them looked down at the access key still sitting in Wing's hand.

"Well, that was embarrassing," Shelby said. "He actually looked slightly disappointed."

☢ ☢ ☢

Otto and Raven walked along the darkened pier. The night air was cold and a thick bank of fog was rolling in off the ocean. There were a handful of lights visible from isolated houses on the hills that surrounded them, but otherwise they were completely alone, the only sound coming from the waves crashing against the shore.

"They're late," Otto said, glancing at his watch.

"They'll be here," Raven said, looking out to sea. Barely a minute later they both heard the high-pitched whine of turbines and a sleek black powerboat raced toward them out of the fog, bouncing across the tops of the waves. It slowed to a stop as it approached the pier and a familiar figure got up out of the seat next to the helmsman.

"Natalya, Otto, it's good to see you both again," Diabolus Darkdoom said, giving them a broad smile. "I hear you've been getting involved in politics. I never really fancied it much myself, such a dirty business."

"Hello, Diabolus," Raven said, taking his offered hand and stepping down into the boat's passenger compartment. "It's good of you to give us a lift. Is the meeting set up?"

"I'll brief you when we're safely onboard the *Megalodon*," Darkdoom said as Otto hopped down into the boat. The three of them took their seats and the helmsman steered them away from the pier. Moments later they were heading back out to sea, the boat's engines whining as it bounced along the surface at phenomenal speed. The ocean ahead of them was lit up by the boat's FLIR sensors, highlighting any nearby vessels or obstacles on the HUD that was projected onto the black glass in front of the helmsman.

"Manta One to *Megalodon*," the helmsman said after a couple of minutes, "we're thirty seconds out. Surface for docking."

Ahead of them the ocean seemed to bulge for a moment and then separate in a shower of spray as the massive conning tower of Darkdoom's stealth submarine, the *Megalodon*, broke the surface. A large hatch in the rear of the tower opened and the helmsman expertly piloted the boat into the brightly lit docking area. Docking clamps thudded into place on the boat's hull as the hatch sealed shut behind them and the *Megalodon* disappeared once more below the waves. The boat's passengers climbed out one by one onto the narrow gangway that led up to the dock.

"We're underway, sir," one of Darkdoom's men reported. "We should reach our destination on schedule."

"Very good," Darkdoom said. "I'm heading to the bridge with our guests. Please make sure that their quarters are ready."

"Yes, sir," the crewman replied.

Otto and Raven followed Darkdoom as he made his way forward toward the giant submarine's command center. They were making their way through the *Megalodon*'s armory when Darkdoom paused for a moment and beckoned for Otto to come and look at something.

"I think you'll appreciate this, Otto," Darkdoom said. "I call it the Moray." He gestured to a rack of weapons stored within one of the *Megalodon*'s torpedo-loading racks. At the front of the weapon was a smooth black egg-shaped nose that was surrounded by an array of cameras and sensors. Behind that was a long, thin segmented metallic body that ended in a vicious-looking barbed tail.

"You're probably aware of the race to develop intelligent airborne drones for the military," Darkdoom said, gesturing toward the machine. "Well, the Moray is an equivalent device for submarine warfare. Extremely maneuverable and quick, it can be equipped for stealthy intelligence gathering or as a highly versatile assassination device, acquiring and eliminating its target completely autonomously."

"Very cool," Otto said, examining the Moray more closely. He closed his eyes for a moment and reached out for the Moray's onboard systems. He could feel the hum and buzz of the *Megalodon*'s other systems, but the weapon in front of him was just dead space as far as his unusual senses were concerned.

"Fully electromagnetically shielded as well," Darkdoom said with a wry smile, "immune to all known counter-measures, including young men with organic supercomputers lodged in their brains."

"So I see," Otto said, raising an eyebrow. "You know it's almost like people don't want me interfering with their highly advanced experimental weapon systems these days."

"How very inconsiderate of them," Raven said. "Now, if you boys have finished admiring your new toys, we do have things we need to discuss."

"You really have no appreciation of craftsmanship, Natalya," Darkdoom said. "I would have thought you of all people would have appreciated a new and interesting way to kill someone."

"I prefer the personal touch," Raven replied, putting her hand on the hilt of one of the twin katanas that were strapped across her back. "You know that."

They continued forward to the bridge which was, as usual, filled with the quiet bustle of a well-trained crew performing its duties. Darkdoom walked quickly around the dimly lit room, checking several gauges and the readouts on key displays. He spoke briefly to his first officer and then gestured for Raven and Otto to follow him through the hatch into his office.

"Everything is in place," Darkdoom said as he closed the door. "The Architect has agreed to a meeting. It took some persuasion, but we've known each other for a long time and he owed me a favor. Be warned though, he is not pleased about being dragged into this conflict, so there is no guarantee that he'll be willing to help us."

"There's only one way to find out," Otto said. "So where are we meeting him?"

"Venice," Darkdoom replied. "Tomorrow afternoon. Piazza San Marco."

"Isn't that a little too public?" Raven asked.

"It was his choice," Darkdoom said. "It was hard enough getting him to agree to the meeting in the first place, so I thought it best not to start questioning his choice of location."

"Does he know what we need?" Otto asked.

"No," Darkdoom replied. "I thought it would be best if we discussed the situation face-to-face. It may be the only chance we have of obtaining the information we require."

"There are other ways of getting information out of someone you know," Raven said. "Given time."

"No, Nero doesn't want him harmed," Darkdoom said, shaking his head. "He either gives his help willingly or we find another way to track Furan down."

"We don't have any other leads at this point," Otto said. "We may never get another chance."

"I understand exactly what's at stake here, Otto," Darkdoom said. "At this point I don't even know if my own son is alive or dead, but Max is calling the shots on this and I trust his judgment."

"So he's agreed to meet with you and Raven's there as security," Otto said. "So how are you going to explain who I am and why I'm there?"

"By telling the truth," Darkdoom replied matter-of-factly. "That you were one of the only survivors of Furan's attack on the Hunt and, as such, one of the only eyewitnesses to her crimes."

"You really think that's going to make a difference?" Otto asked.

"It certainly can't do any harm," Darkdoom replied. "We have to show him that Furan needs to be stopped no matter how important his neutrality is to him. You can help prove that to him."

"I hope you're right," Otto said, "because it might just be our only chance."

81

Anastasia Furan walked through the airlock and into the laboratory area with two nervous-looking scientists in white lab coats trailing behind her. She surveyed the room and seemed satisfied with the level of bustling activity. Technicians hurried about, monitoring workstations and readouts; there was an atmosphere of hurried but not panicked work. At the far end of the laboratory was a sectioned-off area contained within a thick Plexiglas box. Inside the box a large robotic arm was making quick precise movements, working on something that lay hidden within a cloud of white vapor that filled the lower half of the box.

"Is the prototype ready?" Furan asked.

"Very nearly," the older-looking of the two scientists replied. "A couple more weeks of testing and we should be ready for deployment."

"We don't have a couple more weeks, Dr. Klein," Furan said, turning toward him with a slight frown on her face. "I want it ready for deployment now. My sources within G.L.O.V.E. have provided me with some very useful information and I wish to take advantage of the opportunity that it affords us. That opportunity is finite, Doctor, and I will not allow us to miss it because you wish to conduct more tests. Now, I will ask you only one more time. Is it ready?"

"Yes," Klein replied, avoiding eye contact with Furan, "it's ready."

"Good," she replied. "Prepare it to be put into the field immediately. We will need to move the moment that we have a firm target location."

"Understood," Klein said with a nod before walking quickly toward the technicians near the vapor-filled box and engaging them in urgent, hushed conversation.

"Now, Dr. Ross," Furan said, turning toward the other man, "I believe you have work to do."

"Yes, of course," the other scientist replied. "If you'd just follow me."

He led Furan through a nearby door and into another section of the laboratory. He walked over to a steel cabinet with a keypad on the front and punched in a series of numbers. The cabinet popped open with a hiss and he reached inside, pulling out a metal case. He carried the case over to one of the metal tables in the center of the room and opened it as Furan approached. Inside was what looked like a thin skeletal hand made of gleaming steel.

"We are ready to carry out the procedure whenever you are," Ross said, gesturing toward the box. "I should warn you though that you will need to remain fully conscious throughout the procedure so that we can be sure that the neurotech grafting has taken correctly. It will be extremely painful."

"You need not concern yourself with that, Dr. Ross," Furan said, carefully pulling off the black leather glove and revealing the hideously scarred claw that was all that remained of her right hand after Otto Malpense had severely injured her just a few months ago. "I know all about pain."

☻☻☻

Otto, Raven, and Darkdoom walked across the bustling Piazza San Marco, the heart of Venice, trying as much as possible to blend in with the crowds of tourists. Darkdoom was, as usual, wearing a perfectly tailored dark suit and shirt and looked every inch the well-dressed local. Raven had swapped her customary, rather conspicuous, tactical outfit for a pair of tight black jeans, a high-necked sweater and a long dark trench coat. She had, with great reluctance, left her swords onboard Darkdoom's boat, which was moored nearby. They had, after all, no desire to attract the attention of the *Carabinieri*—tangling with the local police was an additional complication that they did not need. Darkdoom took a seat at a table in front of one of the many pavement cafés that surrounded the square and Otto and Raven followed suit.

"Now we wait," Darkdoom said, as a waiter walked over to their table and offered him a menu, which he waved away. "*Solo un caffè per me per favore.* Do either of you want anything?"

"Just water," Raven said, her eyes flicking from person to

person in the crowds that milled around the square, constantly watching for any sign of a hidden threat.

"No, I'm fine, thanks," Otto said.

"*Un caffè e una di acqua, grazie signore,*" the waiter said with a nod and walked away.

Otto took the opportunity to appreciate some of the magnificent architecture that surrounded them, dominated by the spectacular ornately decorated marble arches of St. Mark's Basilica and the towering red brick Campanile opposite it. The most striking thing for a place this busy was the lack of traffic noise; instead there was just the burbling white noise of humanity as a hundred different conversations went on around him.

"He's late," Raven said.

"Maybe, but the important thing is that we're not," Darkdoom replied. "Don't worry, he'll be here."

They had been waiting for several minutes when a voice behind Otto said, "Do you mind if I sit here?"

"Actually we're waiting for someone," Raven said, her hand slipping inside her coat.

Otto turned to see a young woman standing behind him with long dark hair which was held back in a bunch, skewered by a pair of pencils. She was wearing a pair of thick-rimmed glasses, paint-spattered blue jeans and a battered khaki army surplus jacket that looked like it had probably been through at least a couple of wars.

"Oh, I know you are," the girl said with a smile. "My name's Gretchen and you're here to meet with the Architect. I'm going to take you to him."

"Why the change of plan?" Darkdoom asked, with a slight frown. "I thought we were meeting him here."

"Oh no," the girl called Gretchen replied, "much too public. He just wanted you to come here so that I could meet you and confirm that you actually are who you say you are."

I am detecting an encrypted narrow-band signal, H.I.V.E.mind said inside Otto's head. *It would seem to be originating from this young woman.*

Otto noticed the tiny hole in the center of the peace-symbol badge that the girl was wearing on her coat and he reached out with his senses, trying to see if he could determine who might be receiving the signal broadcast by the microcamera that Gretchen appeared to be wearing. It was no good—he could sense the stream of data that was being sent, but after a short distance it was lost in the digital background noise of the hundreds of smartphones, tablets, and laptops carried by the people that surrounded them.

"Understood," Gretchen said after a few seconds, as if replying to someone. "Okay, let's go."

"Go where?" Raven asked.

"That would be telling," Gretchen replied. "Come on, he doesn't like to be kept waiting."

With that, she set off across the square and Darkdoom rose to follow her.

"I'm not sure this is a good idea," Raven said as she and Otto stood up. "She could be leading us anywhere."

"Between the three of *us*," Darkdoom said with a wry smile, "I'm reasonably confident we should be able to handle whatever situation might arise."

They followed Gretchen across the square as she made her way through the crowds.

"We'll take your boat, if that's okay?" Gretchen said as they walked.

"Of course," Darkdoom replied. "Do we have far to go?"

"No, not really," Gretchen said.

Minutes later they were onboard the sleek black boat, sweeping along one of the ancient city's many canals. Otto sat quietly, memorizing their route as Gretchen gave Darkdoom occasional directions. Eventually they pulled into a narrow waterway flanked on either side by the walls of the surrounding buildings. Ahead of them was a darkened tunnel entrance, sealed by a pair of rusty iron gates that slowly swung open as the boat coasted forward.

"Head inside please," Gretchen said, gesturing toward the open gateway. Raven shot Darkdoom a concerned look.

"Nice place for an ambush," Raven said, eyeing the pitch-black tunnel suspiciously.

"If that's how you feel, you can drop me off now and walk

away," Gretchen said with a shrug. "You requested this meeting, remember."

"It's okay, Natalya," Darkdoom said calmly. "We'll be fine."

He pushed forward on the throttle and the boat glided into the tunnel. The gates swung shut behind them and lights flickered on, illuminating the crumbling brickwork of the tunnel which stretched ahead into the gloom.

"Stop the boat," Gretchen said. Darkdoom did as he was instructed and cut the engine, letting the boat slowly drift to a halt. Gretchen reached inside her coat and in a blur Raven had a pistol leveled at the girl's forehead.

"Diabolus," an amplified voice crackled from a loud-speaker mounted on the wall nearby, "please tell your nervous friend to put her gun down."

Darkdoom reached out a hand and placed it on top of Raven's weapon, slowly pushing it downward until it pointed away from Gretchen.

"Hello, old friend," Darkdoom said. "I've been looking forward to seeing you again."

"All in good time, Diabolus," the voice replied. "First, I need you to do what Gretchen here asks you. Please forgive my caution. I fear that I may have become somewhat para-noid in my old age."

Gretchen pulled her hand out from inside her coat and opened it to reveal a tiny black box. She opened the box to reveal three small capsules.

"Please take one each and swallow it," Gretchen said. "The drug inside the capsule is harmless, but it will render you unconscious for approximately half an hour, during which time I will take you to my employer."

"This is too risky," Raven said, shaking her head.

"Then you should feel free to leave and we will go our separate ways. I shall not trouble you and you shall not trouble me, ever again," the voice from the loudspeaker said calmly.

"Natalya, I know this may seem foolhardy," Darkdoom said, "but we have no choice. You may not trust these people, but I know this man. We have nothing to fear from him."

Raven looked Darkdoom in the eye and after a couple of seconds she sighed, gave a tiny shake of her head, and holstered her pistol. Darkdoom reached out and took one of the capsules and handed it to Otto before taking one for himself. Raven took the last pill and placed it in the palm of her other hand, still eyeing it with suspicion. Darkdoom popped the capsule into his mouth and swallowed, followed by Otto and finally Raven. For a few seconds Otto felt nothing, but then he felt a sudden rush of dizziness and the world around him faded first to gray and then to black.

Laura stood behind a pillar at the edge of the combat training area in the bottom of the Glasshouse's central pit, watching for any sign of a guard who might realize that she wasn't actually supposed to be there. She'd arranged to meet Nigel, Tom, and Penny there earlier that morning by discreetly passing them notes during breakfast. The notes had been written on scraps of paper so tiny that they were easily swallowed once read. It would be suicide to be caught by one of the guards with anything that even hinted at any kind of covert conspiracy. It had taken Laura several days of subtle observation to find a spot that was not covered by any of the many cameras that filled the facility. They could meet here unobserved as long as they avoided any random guard patrols. It was the usual hour for the Glasshouse's inmates to carry out their work assignments and she had noticed that the guards seemed to focus their attention on the areas that contained potential improvised weaponry like the kitchen or the workshops during that time. If they were quick, careful, and a bit lucky, they should avoid detection.

Tom was the first to arrive a couple of minutes later.

"I can't stay long," he whispered. "I'm supposed to be cleaning shower block D."

"Is Penny coming?" Laura asked, looking around nervously.

"She'll be here," Tom replied. "She's on laundry duty though, so she needs to make her pick-ups first."

"Hi, guys," Nigel said as he arrived. "Is it safe to talk here?"

"As safe as anywhere is in this place," Laura replied.

"That's not terribly reassuring," Nigel said with a weak smile.

A minute or so later Penny arrived, pushing a cart of dirty laundry in front of her which she parked against the wall before quickly walking over to them.

"I've got five minutes before someone notices I'm taking too long with the collections," Penny said, "so what's this all about?"

"I have an idea for how we can get a message out of here," Laura said, "but I'm going to need your help."

"Okay, I'm listening," Penny said. "What you got, Laura?"

"This might sound crazy, but I need to get access to one of the camera drones," Laura said.

"You're right, that does sound crazy," Tom said with a frown. "They'll execute all of us the moment we lay a finger on one of those things. Not to mention the fact that there's the whole 'they can fly and we can't' thing."

Penny put a hand on his arm. "Let's hear her out," she said. "Assuming we could get our hands on one of those things, what then?"

"I think I can reprogram one with a simple virus that will be transmitted throughout the camera drones and via them to the central server. If I can, I should be able to encode a simple message within that virus that can be hidden inside every data packet that leaves the central server. We wouldn't necessarily know where the message was being sent, but since it would be contained within *every* data packet it would hopefully spread far and wide before anyone realized it was there."

"Then what? We just wait for someone to intercept one of these messages and hope it's someone friendly?" Tom asked. "Seems risky. What if it's decoded by someone else and Furan finds out?"

"Then I'm dead," Laura said matter-of-factly, "but at this point I'd rather risk that than just stay here slowly losing the will to live."

"So it's a message in a bottle," Nigel said.

"Effectively, yes," Laura replied with a nod. "I know it's a long shot, but it's got to be better than nothing."

"So where do we fit into all of this?" Penny asked.

"I need you guys because there's one thing that I have to get for this to work—and only you can get it for me."

chapter five

Flack studied the latest status reports with a mixture of anger and frustration. He had always known that it was probably a vain hope that they would pick up some trace of Malpense at a border crossing, but he couldn't shake the feeling that the mysterious boy had once again slipped the net. He had reviewed the file on Malpense for what felt like the thousandth time and still he was no nearer to understanding who he was or where he came from. There were some records from an orphanage in London giving details of the boy's younger years, but at the age of thirteen he appeared to have simply vanished off the face of the earth. That wasn't terribly unusual; people disappeared all the time, but the fact that he then went on to be involved in events of such magnitude told Flack that there was probably much more to the disappearance than there initially seemed to be. He didn't like mysteries, he liked solutions.

There was a ping from his laptop and he put the file down and focused on the screen in front of him. The supercomputer buried beneath Langley that was responsible for all of the agency's facial-recognition processing had raised a flag. He pulled up the image that had caught the machine's attention and studied it. At first glance it was nothing of interest, just a photo that an English schoolgirl had uploaded to a social-media site showing her and her friends standing in the middle of a busy square. The machines at CIA headquarters routinely scanned all images uploaded to these sites for persons of interest and though the software was good it was notorious for throwing up false positives. The rectangle highlighting the positive hit in this particular image was not framing anyone in the foreground though. Instead it drew his attention to a face in the background. Sitting at a café table behind the group of laughing girls was the woman who the security camera had caught entering the hotel in Phoenix and sitting next to her, with his back to the camera, was someone with a crop of spiky white hair. Flack felt his heart rate increase as he accessed the data embedded within the photograph, silently praying that it had been taken with a smartphone. A moment later his prayers were answered as he studied the properties of the file and saw the precise GPS coordinates that had been recorded at the moment when the photo was taken. He smiled to himself as he punched the coordinates into his laptop's mapping software. His job was so much easier now that everyone carried a device around in their pocket that allowed people like him to track their movements twenty-four hours a day. A second later he had the precise location of where the photograph had been taken less than forty-five minutes ago. He picked up the phone and quickly dialed a number.

"This is Flack," he said, "get me the Italian field office. I want a full snatch team mobilized and feet on the ground in Venice within half an hour. Malpense was in St. Mark's Square less than one hour ago."

☻ ☻ ☻

"I knew he wasn't just lying on a beach somewhere," Shelby said with a grin as she, Wing, and Franz read the report on the screen in front of them. It detailed Otto and Raven's efforts to track down and interrogate the senior members of the Disciples. "Although, with his complexion, lying on a beach for more than about thirty seconds would potentially be just as dangerous as what he's been getting up to. He's been working with Raven all this time."

"It would appear so," Wing said, "though they do not appear to have made an enormous amount of progress." A note of frustration was clearly evident in some of the latest reports. The last update detailed the accidental death of a senior Disciple commander in London while he was being pursued by Raven. Shelby pulled up the accompanying photographs.

"Ewwww," she said, before hurriedly closing the pictures again. "Train one, bad guy zero."

"Yes," Wing said, "most unpleasant, but that was several weeks ago. This file is not up to date."

"Well, at least we are knowing that Otto is okay," Franz said. "That's something, isn't it?"

"Hmmm," Wing said, walking across the room and sitting down on the edge of what had once been Laura's bed, with an unhappy look on his face.

"Hey, you want to give us a minute, Franz?" Shelby said quietly, looking slightly worried.

Franz saw her expression and gave a quick nod before heading out of the room.

"You okay, big guy?" Shelby asked as the door hissed shut behind Franz.

"No, not really," Wing replied.

"What's up?" she asked, putting her arm around his shoulders.

"I hate this," Wing replied, shaking his head and staring at the floor. "Hard as it was when Otto told us that he had been expelled from H.I.V.E., at least we had the consolation of knowing that he would not be in any further danger. But this," he gestured toward the text on the screen across the room, "knowing what he's doing out there makes being stuck here unable to help worse. Otto is more than just my friend, Shelby, he is my brother and I cannot stand the thought of him risking his life trying to find Laura, Nigel, and the others without my . . . without our help." He let out a long sigh.

"Hey, it's okay," Shelby said, hugging him. "I understand, you know. You think there's an hour that goes by without me thinking about Laura? Wondering if she or Nigel are still alive? What Furan did to us . . . it hurts, but we can't . . . we mustn't give up hope."

"I know that, but I just want to help somehow. I'm sick of sitting here, not knowing what's happening. I thought that knowing what progress was being made to find the others would help, but it doesn't. If anything, it just makes it harder."

"Well," Shelby said with a crooked smile, "look at it this way. If you're a member of the Disciples right now, you have Otto tracking you down and Raven coming after you when he does."

"Actually," Wing said, "when you put it like that, I almost . . . *almost* . . . feel sorry for them."

☢ ☢ ☢

Furan slowly flexed her hand in front of her, examining the silver metal that was now fused with her flesh and bone.

The procedure had been quick, but excruciating, just as she had been warned it would be. It didn't matter, she had experienced worse.

"Mobility seems good," Dr. Ross said, examining the screens nearby. "You should find that your grip strength is actually higher than it was before your injury."

"Excellent work, Doctor," Furan said, "thank you. Now if there is nothing else I have pressing matters to attend to."

"No," Ross replied, "just let me know if you experience any problems with fine motor control."

Furan nodded and walked out of the room and into the main laboratory area. She headed toward the rear of the room and examined the large Plexiglas cube. The robotic arm was now immobile, folded into its rest position, and the vapor that had previously filled the room was gone, revealing the empty metal table bolted to the floor in its center. Furan heard footsteps behind her and turned to see Dr. Klein approaching, looking tired but satisfied.

"I assume the prototype is in transit?" Furan asked, glancing over her shoulder at the empty cube.

"Yes," Klein replied, "the transport left over an hour ago. It should be at the target area in less than three hours."

"Good," Furan replied, "and the kill-switch is armed? I want to be able to destroy it if we lose control for any reason."

"Of course," Klein replied, "armed and keyed to your biometric data as requested. Let's hope that we don't have to use it though."

"Indeed, Doctor, let us hope not, for your sake."

Klein swallowed nervously.

"Assuming that this trial goes as planned you may begin the transfer of your equipment and staff over to the main facility," Furan said. "If the prototype is a success, I see no reason to delay Absalom any further."

"As you wish," Klein replied with a nod. "I shall make the necessary preparations immediately."

☹ ☹ ☹

"Otto," Raven said, shaking him gently by the shoulder. "Otto, wake up."

Otto groaned softly and then opened his eyes. He had a slight headache and his mouth was dry, but other than that he didn't seem to have suffered any ill effects from whatever drug it was that they had been forced to take.

"Can anyone tell me what exactly would have been wrong with a good old-fashioned blindfold?" Otto asked.

He sat up and took in his surroundings. He was sitting on a battered leather couch that was on one side of an enormous red-brick structure like a warehouse. The walls of the vast space were covered in hundreds of architectural drawings and technical diagrams. On every flat surface were scale models of buildings, or pieces of machinery. Otto spotted one model that was suspended in midair and realized that he had seen it before. He got up and walked toward the dangling miniature and inspected it more closely.

"This is the orbital platform that Number One . . . that Overlord took me and Nero to," Otto said, eyes wide.

"Orbital platform?" a voice behind Otto said. "Call it what it is, boy, a space station."

Otto turned to see an old man with a cane walking toward him. He had long white hair tied back in a ponytail and a neatly trimmed but full beard and piercing blue eyes. It was hard to tell his precise age, but he was clearly very old, though any physical infirmity that age had brought did not extend to the fire of intelligence that Otto could see dancing behind his eyes.

"A space station, yeah, sorry," Otto said.

"That's the problem with villains these days—always afraid to do something with a bit of imagination. Everything has to be *grounded in reality*, no ambition, I tell you. One of your lot," he gestured at Darkdoom with his cane, "even told me last year that he didn't want an undersea base because it was . . . and I quote . . . unrealistic. Unrealistic! I told him that if he wanted realism he should have hired Norman bloody Foster. No imagination."

The old man stood next to Otto and pointed up at the model of Overlord's space station with his cane.

"One of my most challenging projects actually," the man said. "The design wasn't that hard, but getting an orbital construction crew together was murder. Zero G construction isn't something that it's easy to get a lot of experience in. Thank God for the collapse of the Russian space program, that's all I can say. Shame you had to go and destroy it, young man, but that's the way with these things, I suppose. Tell me though—did it explode well? It's very important that a villain's base should explode well, that's the main thing."

"Erm . . . spectacularly well," Otto replied, looking slightly bewildered.

"Oh, don't look so surprised. I know all about you, Mr. Malpense," the man said. "Quite the reputation you've made for yourself over the past couple of years. You just keep blowing up those bases, young man. It keeps me in work. Anyway, allow me to introduce myself. I'm the Architect, which is a slightly pompous title that gives me a bit of dramatic mystique, so you can call me Nathaniel."

"Pleased to meet you," Otto said, still somewhat taken aback.

"And you," Nathaniel said, pointing his cane at her, "must be the infamous Raven. You don't look so frightening to me, quite attractive actually. If only I was a half-century younger, eh?" He gave her a knowing wink and Otto only realized later that it was the first time he'd ever seen Raven blush.

"You may not have realized it at the time, my dear, but you actually did me a favor a while ago when you killed that hack Nazim Khan," Nathaniel said, patting Raven on the shoulder. "Tried to set himself up as competition, built a couple of bases. Total amateur."

"Actually Sebastian Trent killed him," Raven replied, "to stop him telling me where the secret facility he had built for him was."

"Never did like that Trent fellow," Nathaniel said, shaking his head dismissively. "Don't approve of that whole being a villain but pretending to be one of the good guys thing. Doesn't sit right with me. That's why I refused to build his base for him. That and the fact that he wanted to hide it behind a waterfall. I mean, honestly, what a lack of imagination. I blame video games."

"Hello, Nathaniel," Darkdoom said, a broad smile on his face. "It's good to see you again, old friend."

"And you too, Diabolus," Nathaniel said, smiling back at him. "Lost all the hair now, I see. Not to worry, bald villains never go out of fashion." He turned back to Otto. "Now Diabolus here is a villain after my own heart, my boy, bit of style. You won't find many better role models these days."

"Thank you, Nathaniel," Darkdoom said, "but we do have pressing business we need to discuss."

"We can discuss it over dinner," Nathaniel said, "like civilized human beings. I'll speak to Gretchen and see what she could rustle up. Wonderful girl, very bright, don't know what I'd do without her really."

With that he turned and walked out of the room, leaving Otto, Darkdoom, and Raven feeling like they'd just been the victims of a charming, if slightly rude, whirlwind.

"We don't have time for this," Raven said quietly as she watched him leave.

"Well, we're going to have to make time," Darkdoom replied, "because if there's one thing I've learned about him over the years it's that he can be as stubborn as a mule if he wants to be. We can't rush this. If he decides he's not going to help us then we may never find whatever rock Furan has crawled under."

Otto walked over to the far side of the room and examined some of the pictures on the wall. Some of the blueprints were forty years old.

"I'm assuming you know exactly where we are," Otto said quietly.

Oh yes, H.I.V.E.mind replied inside his head, *and I think you might be surprised to hear what was discussed while you were unconscious. It was really quite interesting.*

"Tell me everything," Otto whispered with a smile.

Flack stood in the center of the darkened control room surveying the bank of flickering monitors in front of him. The agents at the terminals between him and the screens were all talking quickly and quietly into the microphones of their headsets as they worked to coordinate the activities of their men on the ground. Artemis Section's snatch teams were probably the best in the world, hand selected by Flack from the cream of America's black-ops teams. He was confident in their ability; all that he and the agents in this room needed to do now was give them a specific target.

"Think I've got something," one of the analysts nearby said. Flack walked quickly over to her station.

"Show me," he said.

"Here," the analyst said, pointing at CCTV footage of four people walking down one of the streets leading away from St. Mark's Square. It was extremely difficult to get the Italian intelligence services to give access to their security feeds, which was precisely why Flack hadn't bothered asking. Fortunately, he didn't just have the agency's best field agents, he had their best hackers too.

"Well, that's definitely Malpense and the woman from Phoenix," Flack said, studying the image, "but who are the other two?"

The analyst fed the image of the girl's face into the facial-recognition system. A hundred yards below them, some of the most powerful supercomputers in the world began to process the image and compare it to the billions of images that were stored on its system. It broke the girl's features down to simple mathematics, producing a geometrical identifier that was completely unique to her, searching its database for the most likely match. The entire process, that just a decade previously would have taken days or weeks of laborious searching and comparison by eye, took just a few seconds.

"Got her," the analyst said, pulling up a separate window which showed a scan of a passport. "She's Gretchen Metzer, German national, twenty-seven years old, graduated from the D-ARCH Faculty of Architecture in Switzerland, top of her class and then dropped off the grid completely until today."

Flack frowned as another window opened up showing information that had automatically been collated from other systems across Europe.

"Odd," Flack said, studying her file on the screen. "No parental records, no school records, nothing at all before she arrived at college. How exactly did she get into one of the most prestigious architectural schools in Europe without any apparent qualifications?"

"Want me to drill down a little further?" the analyst asked.

"Yes, but first let's see who he is." He tapped his finger on the image of the tall bald man standing next to Malpense.

The analyst fed the image into the system again. A few seconds later a message flashed up onscreen:

CODE VB6

Flack raised an eyebrow. Code VB6 meant that the individual in question was flagged as a Person of Interest by MI6, but that there was no specific data on him in the CIA system. The Agency and their cousins across the water may have cooperated on many things, but there was still some information they didn't share with anyone, even their closest allies. This was just such a person apparently. His frown deepened. He could put in a request for more information, but he suspected that it would get him nowhere and even if he was successful, it would take days. Hacking wasn't an option. British Intelligence's systems were too secure. For now the identity of this man would have to remain as an unanswered question.

"Okay, feed the images of these two new targets to the field team and see if we can find where they were going. The satellite imagery search algorithms should at least have more to work with now that we can add two more targets into the mix."

Flack's prediction was proven to be accurate just a minute later when one of the surveillance satellites that had been re-tasked to the area flagged up a potential match. Flack checked that the time-stamp on the imagery was correct and then studied the saved images. The four targets made their way to a private docking area and boarded a sleek black powerboat. He then tracked the boat's progress as it made its way through the twisting canals before disappearing into what looked like a tunnel running under a group of buildings. He pushed the image and the location coordinates to the ground team controllers' terminals.

"I want eyes on that tunnel," Flack ordered. "I want to know where it leads and if there are any other exits."

Within just a few minutes he had various images up on his screen. The maps of the tunnel system that Malpense had entered were confusing and contradictory. The perfect place to disappear.

"They could be anywhere in there," one of the tactical controllers said. "We could search for a year and never find them."

Flack studied the maps and after a few seconds highlighted a half-dozen locations.

"It may be hard to find someone in a maze," Flack said, "but a maze only has so many exits. I want a blanket thrown over these areas. When they come back out, we'll be waiting."

Otto, Darkdoom, Raven, and Nathaniel took their places around the large mahogany table that occupied the center of the beautifully furnished dining room as Gretchen walked in carrying a steaming stewpot. She placed the pot in the center of the table and took a seat opposite Otto.

"So tell me, Diabolus," Nathaniel said as he helped himself to a ladleful of the stew from the pot, "what is it exactly that you need to discuss with me so urgently?"

"I need your help to find someone," Darkdoom replied, taking a sip from his glass of wine.

"I doubt that very much, Diabolus," Nathaniel replied. "G.L.O.V.E. employs people who are far better suited to finding people than I am. Why aren't you talking to them?"

"Because the person that we're looking for is extremely good at covering their tracks and you may be the only person who knows where they're hiding," Darkdoom replied. "We're looking for Anastasia Furan."

Nathaniel froze, the spoonful of fish stew halfway to his mouth. He lowered the spoon and stared at Darkdoom, his eyes narrowing.

"That's impossible," Nathaniel said. "Furan is dead."

"I'm afraid not," Darkdoom said with a slight shake of the head. "She's very much alive and responsible for recent heinous crimes against G.L.O.V.E. I know I don't need to tell you what she's capable of, Nathaniel. We need your help to find her and stop her."

"I see," Nathaniel replied, frowning, "but what I still don't understand is why you think I can help you."

"You can help by telling us where the training facility you built for her is located," Darkdoom replied. "I know you live by a code of secrecy, Nathaniel, but she is responsible for the murder or kidnapping of dozens of Maximilian's students and we fear that this is only the beginning."

"I'm afraid you've been misinformed, Diabolus," Nathaniel said. "I've never designed any facility for Furan, nor would I have done so if she had approached me. I am quite aware of how dangerous that woman is and even I would draw the line at working for someone like her. You should not confuse my neutrality with a lack of basic morality. Just because I don't take sides doesn't mean I'll happily cooperate with psychopaths."

"Then why did a senior member of her organization tell us that you did?" Raven demanded.

"I have absolutely no idea, my dear," Nathaniel replied calmly. "I would assume, given your involvement, that the information was extracted from him under duress. One can rarely trust what one is told under such circumstances. I'm afraid that you may have been misinformed. Whoever designed and supervised the construction of this facility for Anastasia Furan, it was most certainly not me."

"Oh, it was you all right," Otto said calmly. "You just didn't know it."

"What on earth do you mean?" Nathaniel said, frowning at Otto.

"Do you want to tell him, Gretchen?" Otto asked. "Or should I?"

"What are you talking about?" Gretchen asked, looking slightly bewildered.

"What you may not have realized during our little boat trip earlier was that there were four of us and only three were unconscious," Otto said, placing a silver metal ring on the table in front of him. A moment later a blue wireframe head materialized in the air above the ring.

"Gretchen, meet H.I.V.E.mind," Otto said with a smile. "He's an old friend of mine and he just happened to be listening in to the conversation you had while you were bringing us here. Perhaps you'd like to hear it?"

Otto nodded at H.I.V.E.mind.

"Commencing playback," H.I.V.E.mind said calmly.

"They're here," the recording began, Gretchen's voice unmistakable. "Darkdoom, Raven, and Malpense. They're all incapacitated—do you want me to terminate them?"

"No, we'll wait until all the targets are together," a voice replied with a slight crackle from what must have been a radio of some description. "The team is assembled. We'll eliminate them and the Architect at the same time. He has become a liability."

"Understood," Gretchen replied. "I'll activate the targeting beacon when they're all in one place."

"Which is exactly what you did," Otto said, still smiling, "about two minutes ago. In fact, it's in your jacket pocket right now. H.I.V.E.mind, could you just confirm who our friend here was talking to."

"Voiceprint comparison with archive recordings confirms the other party as Furan, Anastasia," H.I.V.E.mind replied.

Gretchen leaped to her feet and bolted for the dining room door, but Raven was on her in an instant, pinning her to the ground, a knife that seemed to appear from nowhere pressed to her throat. Nathaniel rose to his feet with a dark look in his eye as Raven dragged Gretchen back to her feet, twisting her arm behind her back viciously and making her gasp in pain.

"Two years," Nathaniel said, "two years I've been training you as my apprentice and this is how you repay me. Why? What did Furan offer you?"

"Talk," Raven said, wrenching Gretchen's arm upward, "or I start breaking bones and that's just the start."

"You stupid old fool," Gretchen hissed at Nathaniel through gritted teeth. "She didn't have to offer me anything. I was working for her all along. You were just an assignment. Do you think it was an accident that we met? That I,

III

the perfect apprentice, happened to come along just days after your former assistant died in a car crash?"

"It was you," Nathaniel said, his voice little more than a whisper. "You killed Claudia so that you could take her place."

"Furan needed you to build the new Glasshouse, but she knew you'd never cooperate if you knew what you were designing or who you were doing it for. So I concealed the true nature of the job. You never have paid enough attention to where the work comes from. That's why you've always needed an assistant, someone you can trust to handle the clients. It was easy enough to hide the true nature of the facility, distracted as you were by the challenge that the job represented."

"My God," Nathaniel said quietly, "the Vault, you're talking about the Vault."

"We don't have time for this," Raven said. "Furan's team will be here any second." She reached into Gretchen's pocket and pulled out the small gray cylinder of metal that she found inside.

"Give me that," Otto said, "I have an idea."

Raven handed the tracking beacon to Otto and he closed his eyes for a moment.

"Okay, let's go," Otto said a moment later, picking up H.I.V.E.mind's holographic projector and slipping it into his pocket along with the tracking beacon.

"You're bringing the tracker?" Darkdoom asked with a frown. "That doesn't seem like a terribly good idea."

"Trust me," Otto said.

In the distance they could all suddenly hear the faint sound of helicopter rotors.

"Nathaniel," Darkdoom said, "you should come with us, you heard what Furan said. She wants you dead. G.L.O.V.E. can protect you. It's not taking sides, it's self-preservation."

Nathaniel looked at Darkdoom for a moment and then gave a small nod.

"And you're coming with us," Darkdoom said to Gretchen. "You and Natalya can have a nice long chat once we get out of here."

"Looking forward to it already," Raven said with a nasty smile.

"This way," Nathaniel said, leading them all across the room and through a hidden door in the wall that concealed a staircase leading down to the flooded tunnels below. Raven frogmarched Gretchen down the stairs, following along behind the others as the sound of the approaching helicopter grew louder and louder. They entered a large vaulted cellar where Darkdoom's boat was moored to an ancient cobblestone jetty and he hopped onboard, taking the wheel and firing up the engine with a throaty roar. Raven forced Gretchen down into one of the passenger seats and pulled a pair of cuffs from the bag containing her equipment stowed in the rear of the boat. She cuffed the girl to the seat and then pulled her tactical harness and twin swords from the bag, slipping her gear on with well-practiced speed.

"I'll be with you in a moment," Nathaniel said, hurrying over to what looked like an electrical junction box mounted on the wall. He opened the cover to reveal a numeric keypad and he quickly punched in a series of numbers. A digital readout above the keypad lit up and began to count down from two minutes.

"Now would be an extremely good time to leave," Nathaniel said, climbing down into the boat. "Unless you've always harbored a secret desire to be explosively vaporized."

Darkdoom didn't need to be told twice and he pushed forward hard on the boat's throttle, sending it roaring across the flooded chamber and into the darkened tunnel on the far side. The HUD in the boat's windshield lit up with a glowing green infrared image of the darkened tunnel ahead of him.

"Take the next left," Nathaniel yelled to Darkdoom over the screaming turbines of the boat's engine. Darkdoom did as he was instructed as Nathaniel plotted a course for him through the twisting maze of tunnels that led away from his home. There was the sudden muffled sound of a huge explosion somewhere behind them and Otto felt a wave of hot air wash over him as the self-destruct charges hidden throughout the structure of Nathaniel's studio simultaneously detonated. It was impossible to know if any of Furan's team had been caught in the blast, but there was no way that they were going to be following them down into the tunnels now, regardless.

"I'm sorry that it came to this, Nathaniel," Darkdoom said.

"It's just bricks and mortar," Nathaniel said. "And you know, I've always rather wanted to do that. I've designed dozens of self-destruct systems over the years, but never actually got to set one off. Quite invigorating. I'm starting to understand the appeal. Besides, there was no way I was leaving all of my records for Anastasia Furan to go nosing through. That information would have been far too dangerous in her hands."

Nathaniel continued to direct Darkdoom through the pitch-black watery labyrinth for a couple more minutes until, ahead of them, they saw the illuminated outline of a gated archway, similar to the one they had passed through earlier. As they approached the gates swung open and the boat shot between them and out onto the building-lined canal beyond.

On a rooftop overlooking the canal, a man with a pair of high-powered binoculars studied the passengers onboard the sleek black boat as it raced past beneath him.

"This is observation post nine to all Artemis Section units," the man said quickly into his throat mic. "Positive ID on targets, heading east at high speed. All units converge and apprehend."

chapter six

The miniature submarine glided silently along the hull of the *Megalodon*, dwarfed by the massive vessel. It had approached undetected by any of Darkdoom's crew and it now drifted down onto the larger vessel's armored hull, attaching itself to its outer skin with a soft thud as its magnetic clamps engaged.

Onboard, the *Megalodon*'s captain and his bridge crew tracked the position of the boat carrying Otto and the others as it made its way through the city's canals, oblivious to the parasitic vessel attached to the outer hull, just a few yards away from them.

"Bring us in as close as you can, helm," the captain instructed. "We need to get them out of there as quickly as possible." He studied the map of the canals as Darkdoom's boat sped through them. There was a limit to how close he could bring the *Megalodon* without risking detection. These were after all some of the busiest waterways in the world.

He began to plot a course toward a potential rendezvous point, trying to pick a route that would make their approach as inconspicuous as possible without them risking running aground.

"What the hell?"

The captain spun around and glared at the crewman manning the *Megalodon*'s fire control station.

"Sorry, sir," the crewman said, shaking his head, "but I'm locked out of my station." The captain looked over his crewman's shoulder at his display. Not only was the station locked, but a new target was somehow being fed into the system. He studied the targeting data for a moment and his eyes suddenly widened in surprise.

"Shut down all weapons systems NOW!" the captain shouted, but it was already too late. From somewhere forward of the bridge there was a series of whooshing sounds.

"Three Moray torpedoes in the water," the fire control officer barked. "All tracking on target. I'm still locked out."

"I don't care what it takes," the captain snapped. "I need fire control back online now, we have to . . ."

His final command was never completed. In the armory below the bridge one of the *Megalodon*'s remaining conventional torpedoes received a single digital command and detonated. The resultant series of explosions ripped the *Megalodon*'s belly open, flooding the interior of the giant vessel in seconds and sending it drifting toward the bottom of the Adriatic, further secondary explosions marking its death throes as it disappeared into the blackness of the deep.

The mini-submarine that had detached itself from the doomed vessel just moments earlier shot away at high speed as the three Moray torpedoes raced toward Venice, relentlessly closing the range to their target.

☢ ☢ ☢

"We've got company!" Otto yelled as Darkdoom wrestled with the speedboat's controls, weaving through the far slower vessels that filled the Venetian canals. The water taxi drivers and gondoliers gesticulated wildly at them, hurling elaborate Italian curses as the powerful boat's wake crashed into them. Behind them, three equally fast-moving boats wove through these scattered vessels in hot pursuit. Darkdoom glanced over his shoulder just in time to see a man in the closest pursuing boat raise a compact submachine gun to his shoulder. He took careful aim and fired a short burst over the heads of Otto and the others. The man at the helm of the lead boat raised a handset to his mouth.

"That was a warning shot," the helmsman's amplified voice barked from the speaker mounted on the front of the boat. "Heave to and surrender immediately or you will be fired upon."

"Who are these guys?" Otto shouted over the noise of the engine. "They can't be Furan's men."

"Why not?" Raven asked, raising her pistol and returning fire, putting a round through the plastic windshield of the lead pursuit boat. It slewed to the left, bouncing over the foaming wake of Darkdoom's boat as the helmsman tried to avoid the incoming fire.

"Why would they be bothering with warning shots?" Otto asked, grabbing the nearby handrail as Darkdoom threw their boat around a corner and onto an adjoining waterway.

"Maybe they're trying to avoid hitting her," Raven said, nodding toward Gretchen.

"I don't think so," Otto said. "Hold on a second." He closed his eyes and tried to concentrate despite being slammed from side to side as Darkdoom plotted his breakneck course through the waterborne traffic ahead of them. He could sense bursts of encrypted data packets that were being transmitted both from and to the pursuing boats, but he could make no sense of them.

Would you like me to attempt decryption? H.I.V.E.mind asked inside Otto's head.

"No harm in trying," Otto replied, as another burst of automatic gunfire hit the water just a few yards from the boat in a shower of spray. It was considerably closer than the first warning shot had been.

"Darkdoom to *Megalodon*," Darkdoom said, holding the

radio handset to his mouth, as he wrenched at the steering wheel and sent the boat veering sideways around another corner. "Come in, *Megalodon*." He frowned, disturbed by the lack of response.

"What's wrong? Are they jamming us?" Otto asked.

"I don't know," Darkdoom said, shaking his head as he wrestled with the controls. "It shouldn't be possible, but . . ."

His sentence was cut short as a black shape leaped from the water directly ahead of them. The Moray drone flew over the boat, its long blade-tipped tail whipping through the air. Otto dived for cover as the razor-sharp tip of the drone's tail slashed through the air where his head had been just a moment before, ripping the headrest of his seat to shreds. Raven turned, pulling one of the swords from her back with her free hand and swiped at the drone as it shot past, taking a chunk out of its armored tail before it disappeared back into the water on the other side of the boat with a splash.

"Was that what I think it was?" Otto asked as he grabbed the handrail and tried to get back to his feet.

"A Moray," Darkdoom replied. "Yes, it was." He suddenly realized that something must have gone terribly wrong on board the *Megalodon* if the Moray had been launched with his boat and its passengers as its target. There was no way that could happen by accident. He quickly tried to establish contact with the *Megalodon* again, hoping that there might be some sort of explanation as to why his own weapons had apparently been turned against him, but there was no reply. He pushed the throttle even farther forward, even though he knew they had no chance of outrunning the submerged drone. Otto tried in vain to sense the Moray's on-board electronics anywhere within the murky water around them, but there was nothing. The drone's electromagnetic shielding was proving just as effective now as it had been when he had first seen it onboard the *Megalodon*.

"Nathaniel!" Darkdoom yelled. "What's the fastest route out of the canals and into the lagoon? I'm going to need to get to open water—we need room to maneuver if we're going to have any chance against these things."

"Take the next left," Nathaniel yelled.

There was a thump from somewhere under the boat and a second later the black segmented tail of the Moray smashed up through the floor, tearing a hole in the bottom of the boat and thrashing around the cabin. Gretchen barely had time to register the threat before the drone's tail lanced toward her. It punched straight through her chest, its bloody tip protruding from the back of her seat, and she slumped forward with a gurgling cough. Raven threw her pistol to the deck, drew her other sword, and sprang toward the segmented metal tentacle as it whipped backward, coiling to strike again. The glowing purple blades scythed through the air, no glancing blow this time, and the severed sections of the Moray's tail clattered to the deck, thrashing uselessly. The stump of the tail withdrew, leaving a gaping hole in the hull. Otto grabbed the back of Gretchen's chair and lifted her head, but even if he'd wanted to help her there was nothing he could have done—she was already dead. Water was starting to pour through the tear in the deck as Raven sliced through the cuffs that shackled Gretchen's limp form to her chair, before rolling her body over the side of the boat. It hit the water with a splash.

"Dead weight," Raven said coldly, with a glance at Nathaniel, who just gave a sad shake of the head. Ahead of them a blue and white boat with the words *Polizia Municipale* on the side powered out of an adjoining canal, trying to block the way. The chaos unfolding on the waterways had clearly drawn the attention of the local police. Darkdoom wrenched at the steering wheel, sending their boat sweeping past the prow of the police boat, missing it by just inches. The sudden maneuver caught Otto off balance and he lost his footing on the rapidly flooding deck, toppling over the side and hitting the cold, dirty water in a shower of spray. The impact knocked all the air from his lungs and he struggled to right himself beneath the surface of the murky water. As he kicked his legs, swimming for the surface, something dark shot through the water beneath him, just a few yards away. As his head appeared above the waves, Otto heard an enormous crash from behind him. His head whipped around to see the blazing wreckage of one of the boats that had been pursuing them. It had plowed straight through the police boat and was now bouncing across the water toward him. A split second before it hit him something yanked hard at his legs and pulled him back below the surface. Otto struggled desperately as he saw the burning wreckage crash into the surface of the water just a couple of yards above him. He looked down and was horrified to see the tail of another Moray hunter killer coiled around his ankles, the machine's weight dragging him inexorably down into the murky depths of the canal, the lifeless red eyes of its sensor package staring up at him. He felt his lungs burning as sinking chunks of debris from the destroyed boat began to slowly drift down past him. He thrashed his arms, desperately trying to claw his way back to the surface, but the drone's hold on his legs was too strong and he felt a sudden wave of panic as his strength began to fade. He looked up to the patterns of light dancing across the waves above him. The surface was just a few yards away, but it might as well have been miles. Gray shadows began to dance around the fringes of his field of vision.

Fight, a calm voice said inside his head, snapping Otto back from the brink of unconsciousness.

He saw an oddly shaped piece of debris falling toward him, his oxygen-starved brain taking a second to recognize the shape. He grabbed at the fabric strap attached to the object as it fell past him. It snaked past his fingertips, barely within reach as he made one last desperate lunge for it. He caught hold of the strap and pulled the heavy black weapon dangling from the end of it toward him. Otto grabbed the grip of the submachine gun, aiming it straight at the glowing red lights of the Moray's forward sensor array and pulled the trigger. He felt the weapon jerk in his hand as it fired and the Moray's head disappeared in a cloud of bubbles and sparks, fragments of its delicate tracking equipment tumbling away through the water. He felt the machine's grip on his legs loosen and with his last reserves of strength he pulled his legs free from its limp coils and kicked for the daylight above. He surfaced in the middle of a blazing debris field, taking an explosive gasp of smoke-filled air that nevertheless, in that instant, tasted sweeter than any he had breathed before. He looked around and saw Darkdoom turning his boat around in a tight half-circle fifty yards away, before straightening the wheel and roaring back down the canal toward Otto. He raised one arm, waving frantically to attract their attention, hoping that they would be able to spot him through the smoke billowing from the blazing wreckage of the police boat that blocked the canal behind him. The boat slowed as it approached and Raven leaned out over the side, seizing Otto's outstretched arm and hauling him back onboard.

"Are you okay?" she said, quickly looking him over for any obvious sign of injury as Darkdoom turned the boat back in the other direction and steered them past the burning debris and out into clear water.

"I'll live," Otto said, taking several deep breaths.

"Not far to the lagoon," Nathaniel said, as they raced along between the ancient buildings that bordered the canal. "Next right, Diabolus, and then straight on."

Behind them, another two sleek, high-speed boats shot out from an adjoining canal and continued the pursuit.

"Looks like we've drawn a crowd," Otto said as they raced beneath a bridge filled with tourists watching the drama unfolding in front of them. What the people on the bridge could see, but Otto and the others could not, was the pair of long dark shapes that rocketed along beneath the surface just behind them. A few seconds later Darkdoom's boat emerged from the shadows of the buildings surrounding them and out into the open waters of the Venetian lagoon.

"I still can't establish contact with the *Megalodon*," Darkdoom yelled, pushing the throttle all the way forward. "I think something may have gone very badly wrong."

"Well, we need extraction now, one way or another," Raven replied, looking back at the pair of powerboats still pursuing them across the lagoon. The water in the bottom of the boat was now several feet deep and the extra weight was causing them to slow inexorably.

"You should know I always have a contingency plan, Natalya," Darkdoom said. "We just have to stay ahead of our pursuers for a couple more minutes."

A split second later the water to the left of the boat exploded and a Moray drone flew out of the water and straight at Darkdoom. Raven moved in a blur, the crackling purple blade of her katana sweeping through the air and slicing the machine cleanly in two from nose to tail, one half falling into the water sloshing around the bottom of the boat and the other slipping over the side. At the same instant, the second Moray flew out of the water on the opposite side of the boat and hit Raven squarely in the back, knocking her over the side and into the lagoon. Darkdoom slammed the throttle backward, bringing the boat to a rapid stop as Otto ran to the rear of the boat and looked down into the water. He saw nothing but the faintest glimmer of purple light that seemed to flicker and fade away as he watched. Darkdoom's hand went to the throttle again as he turned and looked back at Otto. The closest of their pursuers was now only fifty yards away.

"We can't leave her," Otto said.

"Nor can we afford to be captured," Darkdoom replied. "I'm sorry, Otto." He pushed forward on the throttle.

"No, *I'm* sorry," Otto said, reaching out with his abilities and blocking the electronic signal from the throttle to the engines. Within just a few seconds their boat was flanked by the two remaining powerboats that had pursued them through the Venetian canals. On each boat, besides the helmsman, there was a pair of men wearing body armor and dark glasses, all with submachine guns raised and aimed at the occupants of Darkdoom's boat.

"No sudden moves, fingers interlaced behind your heads," one of the men barked. "You're all now prisoners of the United States Government."

"I wasn't aware we'd reached international waters," Darkdoom said calmly, glancing at his watch for a split second as he raised his hands and then slowly placed them behind his head as instructed. "I wonder how your friends in the Italian security services would feel about this?"

"I guess we'll just have to make sure that they never find out," the agent replied. He turned to the man next to him. "Cuff them and bring them onboard. I'll call it in."

The two Artemis Section boats edged closer to Darkdoom's vessel as the first agent put a single finger to the side of his neck and spoke into his throat mic.

"Yeah, this is Able Seven. We have the Malpense boy, the male we spotted in St. Mark's Square, and another unidentified elderly male in custody. No sign of the woman though. I can see the retrieval choppers now." In the distance Otto could just make out two helicopters flying low over the water of the lagoon, heading straight for them.

Decryption of their communications is now complete,

H.I.V.E.mind said inside Otto's head. *These men are agents of a branch of the Central Intelligence Agency known as Artemis Section. They report to a director of operations whose name is Flack.*

Behind the agents Otto saw a hand reach up and grab the rail that ran along the side of the Artemis agents' boat. The agent who was talking on the radio started to turn toward the hand clutching the rail; in a second he would spot it and they would be out of options. Otto's mind raced for a moment and an idea formed in his head.

"Let us go," Otto said calmly, "or Flack's dead."

There was a sudden look of surprise on the lead agent's face as he turned back toward Otto, which was swiftly replaced by a look of suspicion.

"What are you talking about, kid?" the agent asked, keeping his gun trained on Otto as his colleague leaned over and grabbed the rail of Darkdoom's boat, pulling the two vessels together.

Behind the two agents Otto saw a second hand on the rail.

"I have an operative in position right now," Otto said calmly. "All I have to do is give her the signal." Otto reached out with his abilities, searching for the capacitor inside the throttle assembly of the other Artemis boat behind him.

"Oh yeah," the agent said with a sneer, "and what kind of signal might that be?"

"This kind of signal," Otto replied and sent a mental command to the throttle capacitor in the boat behind him. The Artemis boat's engine roared, catching its helmsman completely off guard. He was pitched backward, tumbling across the deck, knocking his fellow agents flying as the runaway speedboat powered away across the water, hopelessly out of control. At the very same instant Raven leaped over the side of the stationary Artemis boat, taking advantage of the distraction to surprise the three agents on board. The two agents wielding the submachine guns were the first to go down in a flurry of swift kicks and punches. To the helmsman's credit he managed to get his own pistol halfway out of his shoulder holster before he too joined his unconscious companions out cold on the deck.

"You look like hell," Darkdoom said with a wry smile as Raven took a deep breath. Her tactical harness was gone and her body armor was torn to pieces down one side. She had a long gash that ran down the upper half of her right arm and another similar wound in her thigh.

"Do me a favor, Diabolus," Raven said. "Next time you build yourself something like that thing and its brothers, give them an easily accessible 'off' switch, would you?"

"They *were* designed to be tamper-proof, you know," Diabolus replied, raising an eyebrow.

"Yeah? Well, they weren't me-proof," Raven replied. "And you owe me a new pair of swords. Give me a hand."

She put a hand under each of one of the unconscious agent's arms and dragged him over to the side before rolling him onto Darkdoom's swamped boat. In the distance they could see a small armada of Venetian police boats heading in their direction.

"I'd love to be a fly on the wall in the American ambassador's office when the Italians figure out who these men are," Darkdoom said as he climbed aboard the Artemis boat.

"I always say that it's not really been a good day if you haven't caused a major diplomatic incident by lunchtime," Otto said with a grin.

Otto had just helped Nathaniel across onto the Artemis boat and Raven and Darkdoom were halfway through transferring the last unconscious agent over to their own slowly sinking vessel, when a voice crackled over the agent's radio.

"Able Seven, this is control," the voice said. "Did you say that you could see the retrieval choppers? Because they've only just dusted off—they won't be with you for another ten minutes."

Raven and Otto exchanged a quick glance and then turned and looked at the approaching helicopters. They were much closer and it was now obvious that they weren't designed for transporting personnel. They were clearly gunships, probably the very same ones that would have taken them out at Nathaniel's home if Otto had not realized Gretchen's deception in time.

"I think we need to go," Otto said.

"Yup," Raven replied with a nod.

Seconds later, they were bouncing away across the lagoon, weaving between the sandbanks and mudflats that made navigation of the vast tidal pool so difficult. The boat was no match for the speed of the gunships though and they were relentlessly gaining ground. It would only be a matter of seconds before they were within firing range.

"I hope you have something up your sleeve, Diabolus," Nathaniel said, as they raced toward the gap in the sea wall that led out into the Adriatic Sea. Out here, on the open water, they were sitting ducks.

Darkdoom glanced at his watch and then pulled a small earpiece from his pocket.

"Confirm position," Darkdoom said. He listened for a response and nodded. "Confirm targets, fire when ready."

Nothing happened for a moment and then Otto, Raven, and Nathaniel ducked, flinching as a pair of air-to-air missiles seemed to appear out of thin air just ahead of them and screamed past over their heads straight toward the two gunships. Otto watched as the two pursuing helicopters broke off their pursuit, banking hard as they recognized the danger, but they never had a chance. The burning wreckage of the two gunships tumbled slowly into the lagoon as ahead of the boat there was a shimmering in the air and a giant loading ramp dropped down in midair, hitting the surface of the water in a plume of spray. At the top of the ramp Otto could see the interior of the *Leviathan*'s cavernous cargo hold, the rest of the giant dropship's enormous airframe was rendered invisible by the thermoptic camouflage that covered its armored skin.

"You and your toys, Diabolus," Raven said with a sigh, shaking her head.

"Like I said," Diabolus smiled, "backup plan."

"Most impressive," Nathaniel said, eyebrows raised.

Darkdoom pushed the throttle forward as the *Leviathan* dropped further, its cargo deck flooding with water as its giant invisible turbines kicked up clouds of spray, which in turn revealed the faint outline of its huge hull. Darkdoom steered the boat straight onto the flooded deck and moments later the *Leviathan* lifted back into the sky, Darkdoom's men running forward and stabilizing the beached boat as the water ran off the deck and back into the lagoon below. The huge loading ramp sealed shut as the *Leviathan* continued to climb and Darkdoom, Otto, Raven and Nathaniel got out of the boat.

"Drop this thing in the ocean once we're a few miles out," Darkdoom said to the deck chief, gesturing toward the Artemis vessel. "Who knows what sort of tracking devices it has onboard. Best not to take any chances."

The four of them walked across the cargo bay and up the

stairs leading to the *Leviathan*'s command center. The room was bustling with activity as the operators at various terminals around the room tried to extract any pertinent information from the confused radio chatter that was filling the airwaves of the city below.

"What happened to the *Megalodon?*" Darkdoom asked as he walked to the center of the room.

"We found her automated distress buoy and we'll have Remotely Operated Vehicles onsite shortly, sir," one of the operatives reported. "I'm sorry to have to tell you this, but it appears she's gone down with all hands."

Darkdoom looked down at the floor for a moment and took a deep breath.

"How did it happen?" Darkdoom asked, trying in vain to keep the fury he felt from his voice.

"We're not sure, sir," the crewman replied. "The last telemetry we received from her indicated a catastrophic breach of her fire-control systems, which would tally with the fact she appears to have launched the Moray drones with you and your companions assigned as the primary targets. It seems that she then suffered an on-board detonation of her remaining munitions."

"How is that possible?" Darkdoom asked angrily. "There's no way that anyone could possibly have breached her network security and I am certain of the loyalty of the crew. What the hell happened?"

"We don't know yet, sir," the crewman replied. "We may have a better idea when the ROVs complete their survey of the wreckage."

"Let me know the moment you have the initial report," Darkdoom said, turning to Otto, Raven, and Nathaniel. "We're going back to H.I.V.E. We need to brief Nero and plan our next move. Nathaniel, we need your help. We need to know where Furan's facility is located and what it will take to get our people out."

"I'll help in any way I can, Diabolus," Nathaniel said, "but you must understand that I merely designed the facility. I had no part in its construction. I have no idea where it's located."

"Don't worry," Otto said, pulling the Disciple communicator that they had taken from Gretchen out of his pocket. "I think we might just have that covered."

☻ ☻ ☻

"Okay, here he comes," Laura said, spotting one of the maintenance technicians doing his regular round of checks on the camera drones on the far side of the pit. He was flanked, as normal, by two guards with assault rifles, their faces hidden behind their black Plexiglas masks.

"How long are you going to need?" Tom asked Laura quietly as the pair of them walked along one of the circular balconies surrounding the pit, heading for the first training session of the day.

"I'm not sure," Laura said. "Two minutes maybe."

"Okay," Tom said with a nod. "You're sure Nigel's okay with this?"

"As okay as you could expect him to be under the circumstances," Laura replied. "More to the point, are you sure you're okay with it?" Laura knew that Tom was going to be taking perhaps the greatest risk of all.

"Yeah, what you said before was right. We can't let this place beat the fight out of us." Tom spotted Nigel farther along the balcony and they exchanged a quick glance. "Oh well, I suppose there's no time like the present."

Tom strode toward Nigel, a sudden look of anger on his face.

"Darkdoom!" Tom yelled as he approached the startled-looking Nigel. "I'm going to kill you."

Tom got to within a couple of yards of Nigel, cocked his arm back and punched him squarely in the face. Nigel staggered backward with a yelp, his hands rising to his face and clutching his nose. The two guards began to run along the balcony toward the boys as the maintenance technician and the other students all turned to look at the fight that had just broken out. Laura began to walk away from the fight and around the balcony in the other direction. Tom slammed Nigel against the concrete wall that ran around the balcony, grabbing him by the throat and forcing him backward over the barrier until he was hanging over the fifty-yard drop to the open-air training area at the bottom of the pit. Unseen by anyone, Penny walked past the maintenance technician, whose attention was firmly focused on the unfolding drama and in a quick, fluid movement lifted the PDA from the pouch on his belt. She kept walking, quickly passing the PDA to Laura who shoved it into the pocket of her combat trousers, before ducking back into her cell. She pressed her back against the wall, taking cover behind the door frame and activated the PDA, her thumbs dancing across the touch-sensitive keyboard on the screen in a blur.

Outside, the guards slowed as they approached Tom and he pushed Nigel further out over the lethal drop to the ground below. Nigel had a look of fear on his face, both hands clinging onto Tom's wrist as the other boy held his throat in a vice-like grip.

"Stay away from me," Tom yelled at the guards. "One more step and he's gone. I mean it."

"Okay, kid," one of the guards said. "No one needs to do anything stupid."

The camera drones that had been watching the trainees on that level make their way to lessons, all now hovered with their lenses focused on Tom and Nigel as their operators in the glass control tower, hanging from the ceiling above, analyzed the developing situation. No one noticed as the light on the bottom of one of the hovering drones flickered from green to red.

Laura worked at blinding speed, working through the tools that were installed on the technician's device. She found what she needed—a basic scripting tool for composing diagnostic subroutines—and she started to code, almost falling into a trance as she typed line after line of code, never having to pause for thought. To her, English was her second language; the lines of instructions that scrolled up the screen were written in her true mother tongue and it had been too long since she had been able to speak it.

Meanwhile, guards were now flanking Tom and Nigel on both sides. Tom looked at them as they slowly advanced.

"Keep back," Tom screamed, "or he's dead. I want to speak to Furan."

One of the guards turned away, raising his hand to his ear as he received a transmission inside his helmet. The guard turned back toward Tom.

"You should be careful what you wish for, kid," the guard said. A few moments later the watching crowd parted and Furan, flanked by more guards, strode through the crowd. She stopped ten yards away from Tom, glaring at him with an expression that was a mixture of anger and contempt.

"What are you doing?" Furan growled.

"I want out," Tom said, a slight tremor in his voice. "Let me go or I swear to God I'll kill him. I know who his father is and how important he is to you. Let me go and I'll vanish—no one will ever hear from me again, I swear."

Laura finished typing. There was no time for fixing bugs or checking her code, it had to be right the first time. She hit the transmit button and the new subroutine was uploaded wirelessly to one of the camera drones hovering just outside. A moment later the light on its belly flicked back from red to green. She shut down the PDA and walked back outside, passing the device to Penny as she walked past her. Penny kept walking, watching Tom's confrontation with Furan nervously as she approached the technician who was still watching the drama on the other side of the central chamber. She slipped the device back into the pouch on the man's belt as she passed and he never noticed a thing. The distraction had worked.

"Give me your sidearm," Furan said to one of the guards and the man pulled the pistol from the holster on his hip and handed it to her. She turned back toward Tom.

"Did you really imagine, even for one second, that I was going to let you just walk out of here?" Furan asked Tom, approaching him.

"If you don't, he dies," Tom said, sounding desperate.

"I'm afraid, young man," Furan said, raising the pistol, "that you've seriously overestimated the strength of your negotiating position."

She pulled the trigger and the gun bucked in her hand just once. Tom gasped, his eyes wide with shock, as the bullet struck him in the center of his chest. His grip on

Nigel went slack as his knees buckled and he collapsed to the ground. Nigel clawed at the air frantically as he tipped backward and fell over the balcony wall.

"No," Laura whispered as she saw Tom topple over and Nigel begin to fall. Nigel's arms flailed as he fell, only a thin strangled scream escaping his lips. Ten yards below him there was the sound of an explosive release of pneumatic pressure and a catch net shot out from the wall of the pit, directly beneath him. Nigel hit the net and lay there gasping for breath, his face a mask of fear and shock. Penny ran toward where Tom was lying on the ground, but a guard grabbed her and roughly shoved her back against the wall where she stood sobbing, tears rolling down her face as she watched another pair of guards grab her best friend's arms and drag his lifeless body away.

"Clear the area," Furan said, handing the pistol back to the guard. "I believe that this particular lesson is complete."

☺ ☺ ☺

The *Leviathan* slowly descended into H.I.V.E.'s crater landing bay, the giant aircraft filling the entire area as it settled with a thud on to its landing gear. The loading ramp at the rear of the dropship lowered with a whirring sound and Darkdoom, Otto, and Raven made their way down the ramp with Nathaniel following behind.

"Impressive," Nathaniel said, looking up at the giant

hangar doors that were sliding shut far above them, concealing the hangar hidden within the volcano that was home to H.I.V.E.

"Welcome back," Colonel Francisco, head of H.I.V.E.'s tactical training department, said as he walked toward them. "Doctor Nero sends his apologies for not being here in person to welcome you, but he's in the middle of briefing the G.L.O.V.E. ruling council on the latest developments. Diabolus, he asked if you would join him in the conference room? The meeting is already in progress."

Darkdoom gave a quick nod and walked briskly toward the exit.

"Nero will meet the rest of you in his office as soon as the briefing is complete. Raven, would you be good enough to escort our guest there?"

"Of course, this way please." Raven gestured for Nathaniel to follow her. "You too, Otto."

The three of them walked toward the hangar exit as Francisco supervised the ground crews refueling and rearming the *Leviathan*.

"Mind if we stop by block seven on the way?" Otto asked as the three of them walked up the stairs.

"Maybe later," Raven said. "You'll have to ask Nero."

They walked through the empty corridors of the school, seeing no one but the familiar security guards in their distinctive orange jumpsuits, patroling the hallways for stray students while lessons were in progress. Otto couldn't shake the feeling that something was different about the place. The guards eyed them with suspicion as they passed, despite Raven's presence. There was a subtle tension in the air, almost as if H.I.V.E. was on a war footing, bracing itself for the next attack. He supposed that was not entirely surprising under the circumstances. The attack on the Hunt had been a massive hammer blow to the school after all, and the people who were responsible were still very much a threat.

"I have to confess that I was always rather skeptical about Maximilian's ability to construct this facility," Nathaniel said as they walked past a window looking down into one of the tactical training caverns where, far below them, a group of Henchman students in their blue uniform jumpsuits were storming a large concrete building. Instructors stood around barking instructions at them as they practiced breaching and clearing the structure. "We had something of a bitter falling out over it to be honest. I told him it was a foolish notion to build inside an active volcano and I wanted no part of it. He always insisted that it was viable though. It appears I may have rather underestimated him." He pointed his walking stick up at the lights in the ceiling. "I assume that the whole facility runs on geothermal power?"

"Yes," a familiar voice said behind them, "the hardest

part was controlling the pressure in the magma chamber actually."

They turned to see Professor Pike walking down the corridor toward them, a broad smile on his face.

"Theodore!" Nathaniel said, grinning. "How are you, old friend?"

The two old men embraced, clapping each other on the back.

"I'm very well thank you, Nathaniel," the Professor replied, still smiling, "other than the usual inconveniences of our ever increasing years, of course."

"Don't remind me," Nathaniel said with a chuckle. "It seems like a new and interesting part of my body starts hurting every morning."

"I know the feeling," Pike said. "We still have it where it counts though." He tapped the side of his head.

"Even if you still can't beat me at chess," Nathaniel replied with a wry smile. "Knight to queen's bishop three. Checkmate."

The Professor paused for a moment picturing in his head the layout of the pieces on the board in the latest of the games that the two of them had played over the years.

"Damn," the Professor said after a moment or two, shaking his head. "Thought I had you there too." He turned toward Otto. "It's good to see you too, Mr. Malpense. Staying out of trouble, I hope?"

"Of course," Otto replied. "You know me, Professor."

"Indeed I do, Mr. Malpense, indeed I do," the Professor replied, "which is why I've activated the school's long-range defense grid. Just as a precaution you understand."

"We need to keep moving," Raven said. "Doctor Nero will be finished briefing the council shortly and we shouldn't keep him waiting."

"Of course," the Professor said with a nod. "You should pop down to the Science and Technology department when you're done, Nathaniel. I have a couple of things to show you that I think you might find interesting."

"Looking forward to it," Nathaniel replied with a smile.

Otto, Raven, and Nathaniel moved on, making their way through the twisting corridors until they arrived at Nero's office. Raven placed her hand on the palm scanner next to the door and it slid aside with a soft hiss. Raven stood to one side of Nero's desk as Otto took a seat and Nathaniel moved across the room, studying a Turner seascape painting on the wall.

"I'll be damned," Nathaniel whispered under his breath. "So that's where it ended up."

A moment later the door hissed open again and Nero and Darkdoom walked into the room, both looking serious.

"Good to have you back, Natalya," Nero said with a nod to Raven, "and I'm glad to see that you made it back in one piece too, Otto—though the Italian authorities are rather

144

upset about the incident in Venice. Our local operatives will have to keep a low profile for a while." Nero glanced over at Nathaniel, a curious, unreadable expression on his face as the old man turned slowly to face him.

"Hello, Maximilian," Nathaniel said, a smile tugging at the corner of his mouth.

"Hello, Father," Nero replied.

chapter seven

"I'm afraid that an apology is not always sufficient," Furan said, raising the silenced pistol that had been resting on her lap and leveling it at the startled man on the other side of her desk. The man rose quickly to his feet as the pistol made two soft coughing sounds. The man toppled backward over his chair, hitting the ground with a thud as one final breath rattled from his lungs. The other two men sat facing her glanced at each other nervously as Furan placed the pistol on the desk in front of her, a wisp of white smoke rising from its muzzle. "No apologies, gentlemen, just explanations. Explain to me how we can have such a collection of high-value targets in our sights and yet the only person who was killed was our own operative."

"We're not sure," one of the men replied, licking his lips nervously. He wore a dark suit, his short black hair swept back from a widow's peak. "The last communication we had from the Metzer girl was when you spoke to her. As you know she gave no indication that she had encountered any difficulties."

"And yet our targets made their escape and we lost a hugely valuable opportunity, Mr. Withers," Furan said, her expression unreadable. "Did we achieve anything of value? I assume not on the basis of the late Mr. Sands's tactical report." She gestured vaguely at the body on the floor.

"We did have some success," Dr. Klein replied, shifting uncomfortably in his seat, trying hard to not be distracted by the fresh corpse that lay on the ground next to him. "The prototype performed flawlessly. It was unfortunate that the assassination drones that it launched from the *Megalodon* were ineffective, but it did manage to destroy Darkdoom's vessel and escape entirely undetected. That will be a bitter blow to Darkdoom and his allies."

"Indeed," Furan replied. "You did not encounter any behavioral aberrations, I assume?"

"Nothing but unwavering obedience," Klein replied. "The alterations we made to its personality matrix appear to have been successful."

"Good. Then I see no reason why we should not proceed to the next stage of the operation," Furan said with a satisfied nod. "I take it that everything is ready at the incubation facility?"

"We can begin the process immediately," Klein replied.

"Then do so," Furan said. "Project Absalom is vital to

our future plans, Doctor Klein. Work quickly but carefully. I will be most *displeased*"—she glanced meaningfully at Sands's body—"if anything was to go wrong with the next stage of its development. I trust I make myself clear?"

Klein nodded, swallowing nervously.

"Good. You may go."

Dr. Klein stood up and left the room, walking carefully around the pool of blood that was slowly spreading across the polished-concrete floor.

"Congratulations, Mr. Withers, you are my new head of tactical operations. Let us hope you are more successful than your predecessor," Furan said with a nasty smile. "We should expect retaliation from G.L.O.V.E. for our attack on Darkdoom's submarine. Increase security on our other facilities and make sure that the protection details around the other senior Disciples are at full readiness. I do not want a repetition of the fiasco with Senator Ronson."

"I will double their surveillance and protection details," Withers replied with a nod.

"No mistakes," Furan said. "Very soon our fight with Nero will escalate from a series of skirmishes to a full-scale war and I want to ensure the safety of our assets when it does. Dismissed."

Withers stood and walked toward the door.

"Oh, and Mr. Withers, please arrange a clean-up team,"

Furan said casually, gesturing toward the corpse on the floor, "to deal with this . . . *mess*."

☻☻☻

Otto imagined his own expression was just as surprised as the one on Raven's face as Nero and Nathaniel faced each other. *Father?* Otto thought. *What the hell?* Obviously he knew that Nero must at some point have had parents just like everyone else, but for some reason he still found it difficult to get his head around the concept that Nero had anything as normal as a family.

"Your school is most impressive," Nathaniel said, gesturing at the walls around him with his stick.

"Thank you," Nero said, "though I do seem to remember you telling me that building it would be impossible."

"Yes, well, sometimes I'm wrong about these things," Nathaniel replied, "though not often."

Nero stood behind his desk and Darkdoom took a seat next to Otto.

"So, what exactly have you got me involved in this time, Maximilian?" Nathaniel asked, turning back to study the Turner painting. "You know that I don't take sides in these things normally, but Diabolus tells me that Anastasia Furan has reared her frightfully ugly head again."

"Indeed," Nero replied, "so I had you brought here for your own protection."

"I am quite capable of looking after myself, thank you," Nathaniel said, sounding slightly irritated.

"As clearly evidenced by your excellent choice of apprentice," Nero replied. "An apprentice who it now appears was working for Furan the whole time. What exactly was it that she persuaded you to do?"

"Who I choose to work with is my affair," Nathaniel said with a dismissive wave of his hand. "She was an excellent student and a talented architect. I suppose you're trying to tell me that you've never been betrayed by someone you thought you could trust. Besides, Furan only attacked me when I got involved with your lot."

"It was only a matter of time before she decided that you had outworn your usefulness to her regardless of whether you were working with G.L.O.V.E. or not. I may have always tolerated your neutrality, but Furan expects nothing less than absolute loyalty and obedience."

"Oh, and I suppose your organization is built on a foundation of easy-going camaraderie, isn't it? Do you know why I've always remained neutral in these affairs? I'll tell you why. Because you're all as bad as one another. There was a time when you at least knew where you stood, who you could trust and who you couldn't. Now you're all too busy with double-crosses, betrayal, and squabbling to actually get anything done."

"Gentlemen," Darkdoom said quickly, before Nero could

reply, "this is getting us nowhere. The fact of the matter is that we are now all firmly within Anastasia Furan's sights and we have to find her and her allies and stop them before they can do any more damage. Then we can all take as much time as we like to argue the rights and wrongs of our respective positions, but right now we need to prioritize."

Nero and Nathaniel stood glaring at each other for a moment before Nero sat down behind his desk with an exasperated sigh.

"Can you tell us anything about this new Glasshouse that you designed for Furan?" Darkdoom asked.

"As I've already explained," Nathaniel replied, "I had no idea that was what it was. It was Gretchen who initially brought the project to my attention. She told me that she had been approached by a secretive branch of the Russian intelligence services who wanted me to design a new prison facility for them. It was supposed to be somewhere that they were going to incarcerate the worst of the worst, people who must be kept behind bars indefinitely. It had to be totally secret and most of all it had to be impregnable. We called it the Vault and I took the project on because it was a challenge that I had not encountered before; a truly secure facility that it would be impossible to break out of."

"And you didn't have any reason to suspect that Gretchen was lying to you?" Darkdoom asked.

"No reason at all," Nathaniel replied, shaking his head.

"It was quite normal for her to bring a project like that to me and I've always left my assistants to deal with the relationship with my clients. I didn't want to be bothered with all that. The only thing that was slightly unusual about this particular project was that the client would not discuss the geographical location of the structure. It was slightly out of the ordinary, but it wasn't the first time that I'd worked under those conditions. Sometimes my clients just want a blueprint, sometimes they want me to arrange the entire construction of the project. It's their decision ultimately. They provided me with basic topographical and geological details of the site and I adapted my design accordingly."

"So this Vault was actually Furan's new Glasshouse," Otto said, "and you had no idea that you were working for her."

"No," Nathaniel said with a worried expression. "I would never have taken the project if I'd known, but I had no reason to suspect otherwise. Up until a few hours ago I thought that Anastasia Furan was dead. Nobody had told me about her apparent return from the grave." He raised an eyebrow at Nero.

"I didn't think it would be necessary," Nero replied. "We had no idea that you were working with her. If I'd known I would have had someone contact you and warn you."

"Well, it's a bit late to worry about that," Nathaniel said. "Now we have to try and find where exactly she built this thing. It was designed to house murderers and psychopaths, the worst scum of the earth. The fact that she's keeping children there turns my stomach. We may not see eye to eye on many things, Maximilian, but I *will* help you stop her. It changes nothing between us, but the fact that those children are being imprisoned in such appalling conditions is partially my fault and that is a mistake I intend to put right."

"All of which, unfortunately, leaves us no closer to discovering Furan's location," Nero said with a sigh.

"Actually," Otto said with a wry smile, "that's not entirely true."

He pulled the Disciple communications and tracking device from his pocket, placing the metal cylinder on Nero's desk.

"What's this?" Nero asked with a frown.

"That's the communicator that Gretchen contacted Furan with and then used to guide the Disciple gunships to our location."

"And you brought it here?" Nero said, sounding alarmed.

"Oh, don't worry," Otto said. "I'm jamming it. It's still transmitting, but as long as I'm here and conscious it's not actually sending a signal home."

"How reassuring," Nero said.

"I'm not stupid," Otto replied. "I understood the risk of bringing it here, but it may be the only way we'll find the

Glasshouse. Let me . . . let us . . . explain. One second."
Otto pulled the small silver disc from his other pocket and
placed it on Nero's desk next to the Disciple device. A
moment later H.I.V.E.mind's head materialized, floating in
the air above it.

"Good afternoon, Doctor Nero," H.I.V.E.mind said
calmly. "It is good to see you again."

"H.I.V.E.mind, can you tell us how long it would take us
to decrypt the Disciple carrier signal using conventional
means?" Otto asked as H.I.V.E.mind's hovering head turned
to face him.

"The signal employs biphasic quantum encryption. I
calculate that using the full processing capacity of H.I.V.E.'s
systems it would take nine years, three months, one week—"

"Okay, we get the idea," Nero said impatiently. "So how
does this help us?"

"Because we're going to use more processing power,"
Otto said. "It's going to take a few hours to set up and I'll
need to speak to Professor Pike about some of the details,
but I think there's a way we can crack their code in a matter
of hours. Once we do, it should be relatively straightforward to work out exactly where this thing is trying to
transmit its location to."

"And you believe that's the Glasshouse," Nero replied,
staring at the device on his desk.

"Yes, though we can't be sure until we crack the code,"

Otto replied. "If I'm wrong, it's back to square one. If I'm right, it might be us catching Furan by surprise for a change."

"If we do find the facility's location, we'll need to have an assault plan in place," Raven said, turning toward Nathaniel. "Presumably the blueprints for the Glasshouse were lost when your studio was destroyed."

"Yes, but I have a copy," Nathaniel replied, tapping the side of his head. "I'll need a drawing board and some pencils and paper."

"I can provide you with access to a full suite of CAD and visualisation software if you require it," H.I.V.E.mind said.

"No, I most certainly do not require it," Nathaniel replied, sounding offended. "Amateurs use computers, a professional doesn't need them. Just find me somewhere quiet to work."

"As you wish," H.I.V.E.mind replied with a nod. "I will need to be transferred back to my datacore in order to work at peak efficiency." He turned to Otto. "No offense."

"None taken," Otto said, grinning. The organic super-computer in his head was unbelievably powerful for its tiny size, but it would be much more efficient for H.I.V.E.mind to move back into the school's system for now. "I'll head down there now and you can transfer over."

"Good," Nero said. "It sounds like we have a plan of action. Natalya, will you escort my father to one of the spare teachers' offices and provide him with whatever he needs. Keep me updated on your progress."

Raven nodded and gestured for Nathaniel to follow her.

"Mr. Malpense, you will be needing this if you're going to be staying here for a while." Nero walked over to a tall cupboard on the far wall and pulled out a black jumpsuit, the distinctive uniform of a H.I.V.E. Alpha stream student, from inside.

"I seem to remember that we told everyone that I'd been expelled," Otto said.

"Then I expect you'll want to tell your friends of your reinstatement in person," Nero said, handing the uniform to Otto. He tapped something into the terminal on his desk. "They have just finished their final lesson of the day. I expect they'll be heading back to their quarters." He picked up the Disciple device from his desk and passed it to Otto. "You have work to do, of course, but I'm sure it can wait for an hour or two. Dismissed."

"I'll make sure the *Leviathan* is ready for launch," Darkdoom said, as the door hissed shut behind Otto. "How are you feeling?"

"Fine," Nero said. "It's strange to see him again after all these years. I know that H.I.V.E. is the safest place for him now, but I'd forgotten just how exasperating he can be."

"He's stubborn as a mule," Darkdoom said, smiling. "Rather like someone else I know. You two have more in common than you realize. Though I think Natalya may be slightly annoyed with me that I didn't tell her the whole truth about who Nathaniel was."

"I'll tell her that I asked you not to," Nero said. "I'm sure that she'll understand the situation in Venice was quite complicated enough without the details of my family tree complicating it still further. I was sorry to hear about the *Megalodon*'s crew, Diabolus. I know how much your people mean to you."

"We've all suffered losses, Max," Darkdoom replied. "The real tragedy would be if the people responsible weren't held to account. For now we need to concentrate on getting your students back and making Furan pay for what she's done."

"Oh, she's going to pay, Diabolus," Nero said, a look in his eye that Darkdoom had only seen on a couple of occasions before. "That much I can *promise* you."

☹ ☹ ☹

Otto zipped up the front of his uniform and looked at his reflection in the mirror. It had been months since he'd worn it and he was surprised at how comfortable and familiar it felt. It seemed strange to think now that when he'd first arrived at H.I.V.E. all he'd wanted to do was to find a way to escape. Now it felt like home and it was good to be back. He opened the door of the cubicle and walked out into the changing room. There were a small group of

Henchmen students getting changed after one of their physical training sessions and Otto immediately recognized two familiar, but unwelcome faces.

"I thought we'd finally seen the last of you, Malpense," the hulking shaven-headed Henchman student called Block said with a nasty sneer. The last time Otto had seen Block, the thug had tried to kill him and very nearly succeeded. The other Henchman students turned to face Otto, including Block's half-witted accomplice Tackle.

"Well, I'm back," Otto said with a smile. "Awww, did you and Tweedle-dummer miss me? That's sweet really."

Block advanced toward Otto, his hands balling into fists, but Tackle grabbed him by the shoulder and held him back.

"Remember what Nero said," Tackle whispered. "We touch 'im or any of his friends, we're dead."

Otto turned to leave. He didn't have time to deal with these two idiots right now.

"Count yourself lucky, Malpense," Block snarled. "Nero won't always be around to watch your back, you know."

Otto stopped, his hand on the door handle and then he turned back toward Block. The look on his face alone was enough to send a shiver down a couple of the other Henchman students' spines. They'd heard the rumors about Otto. He could do *weird things* or at least that's what they'd heard. Otto walked straight up to Block and jabbed his finger into the hulking brute's chest.

"No, you drooling moron, count *yourself* lucky," Otto snapped, something cold and hard in his voice. The lights in the room flickered for a moment. "Because I never told Nero what you and this idiot actually tried to do. He doesn't know that you were going to kill me and Laura. I told him you were 'unwitting accomplices' of Harrington and that you weren't really to blame. Here's the thing though. I haven't forgotten what you did or what you were going to do and if I ever think for one second that you're going to lay a finger on me or any of my friends ever again, you're both dead."

"Yeah? What you gonna do, Malpense?" Block said, still sneering. "You gonna go running to Nero?"

"No," Otto replied, his voice like ice. "I'm going to reach inside that thick skull of yours and switch you off. I'm not even really sure if I could do it. It might just leave you brain dead. It might leave you with just enough consciousness to feel each spoonful of baby food that the nurse shoves into your stupid fat face. I don't know and I don't care. You shouldn't be afraid of Nero, you should be afraid of *me*."

Block opened his mouth, but nothing came out. A moment later, he closed it again and swallowed nervously. Otto stared at him for a second and then turned and walked out of the room.

"Do you really fink he could do that?" Tackle whispered nervously as Otto left.

"I dunno," Block said, shaking his head and silently praying to himself that he'd never find out.

⊛ ⊛ ⊛

"Hey, what you guys up to?" Shelby said cheerily as she flopped down onto the couch next to Wing, who was frowning at the piece of paper on the table in front of him. On the paper was a phenomenally complicated diagram that looked like a set of intricately nested flowcharts.

"I am being trying to explain to Wing how G.L.O.V.E. is using the bankers' bonuses as a way of paying operatives," Franz said. "It is being quite simple really, but I am not being sure if I am making it clear enough."

"Your explanation has been quite clear, thank you, Franz," Wing said, still frowning. "I just think that financial corruption on this scale may be a little more than I can get my head around."

"Poor old ninja boy," Shelby said, smiling. "Knows twenty-seven ways to take you down with just his pinky, but can't actually count to twenty-seven."

"So this makes perfect sense to you, I suppose," Wing said, handing the sheet to Shelby.

"Yeah, it's easy," Shelby said, pointing out one area of the diagram. "See this piece here is just gobbledegook." Her finger moved to another area. "Whereas this section is premium-grade incomprehensible gibberish and this section," her finger moved again, "appears to be mostly in Greek."

"Am I to take it that you have not studied for the test tomorrow at all then?" Wing asked, raising an eyebrow.

"Nope," Shelby said with a grin. "There's going to be some good old-fashioned last-minute cramming later though. Either that or I'm going to just sit near my best bud Franz here and he's going to write out all the answers in nice, b-i-i-i-g, easily legible letters. Right, bud?"

"This is being what I normally do,' Franz said with a sigh, "isn't it?'

"You could always try studying for a change," Wing said, taking the incomprehensible diagram back from Shelby.

"Yeah, but where's the fun in . . . oh my God!" Shelby's eyes widened in shock and a huge grin appeared on her face as she spotted something over Wing's shoulder. She instantly leaped to her feet and began sprinting across the atrium. Wing turned and looked behind him, a look of bewildered surprise on his face, trying to see just what had provoked her reaction. Standing in the entrance of accommodation block seven was a boy with snow-white hair.

"Otto!" Wing yelled and he too jumped up, running toward his friend. Otto braced himself as Shelby hit him at high speed, almost knocking him clean off his feet, hugging him and squealing at a pitch that was normally only audible to dogs.

"OhmyGod, OhmyGod, OhmyGod," Shelby said after a second, talking incredibly quickly. "What are you doing here?" She grabbed him by the shoulders and looked him up and down with tears in her eyes, as if checking that he was actually real. She stepped back as Wing reached his friend and wrappped him in a back-breaking bear hug, lifting him off the ground and laughing.

"Whoa there, big guy," Otto said, grinning. "I've only got the one spine, you know."

"Otto, it is so good to be seeing you," Franz said, jogging up to the others as Wing put his friend back down on the ground.

"Where have you been? What have you been doing? When did you get back? Aren't you expelled? Are you unexpelled?" Shelby asked, apparently unconcerned with breathing.

"My friend," Wing said, smiling from ear to ear, "it is so good to see you."

"You too, Wing, you too," Otto said, suddenly feeling as if a massive weight had somehow been lifted from his shoulders.

"Are you back for good?" Shelby asked, oblivious to the crowd of students in the atrium who were all suddenly looking in their direction.

"I'm back for now," Otto said, his expression suddenly becoming more serious. "I'm afraid there's good news and there's bad news. Come on, let's sit down and I'll tell you all about it."

The four of them walked back to the sofa and sat down. Otto explained exactly where he had been for the past few months and exactly what it was that he'd been doing. He explained how they now had an idea where Laura and the rest of the captured Alpha students were, but that there was still a lot that needed to be done before they might be in a position to rescue them.

"So that's why H.I.V.E.mind has been offline all this time," Shelby said as Otto finished. "You had big blue rattling around inside your noggin again the whole time."

"Well, he's not there right now," Otto said, tapping the side of his head. "He's back in the school datacore, but yeah, he's been along for the ride the whole time."

"So how long before we can mount a rescue operation?" Wing asked.

"Hopefully not long," Otto said, smiling at his friend's assumption that they would all be going to find their friends. "I need to spend some time with H.I.V.E.mind and see if we can crack the encryption on the Disciple beacon. If we can, we can begin tactical planning immediately. If we can't, well, frankly, we're back to square one."

"Do you think it'll work?" Shelby asked. "You think you're going to be able to work your mojo on this Disciple gizmo?"

"Honestly, I'm not sure," Otto said. "We'll see. It depends on whether or not my plan for cracking the encryption is sound. The theory's good, but theory's one thing, practice is another."

"Is there anything we can do to help?" Franz asked.

"Not right now, but if we do find out where the Glasshouse is I want you with me when we go in. Not just because you're my friends, but because you also just happen to be the best damn infiltration team I know."

"Just try and stop us," Shelby said. "I've been getting cabin fever without you around to get us into trouble."

"Awww, never knew you cared, Shel," Otto said with a wink.

"You think Nero will allow us to come with you?" Wing asked with a slight frown. They all knew that Nero was notoriously reluctant to deliberately place his students in harm's way.

"Yeah, I do," Otto replied.

"And why is that?" Wing asked.

"Because I have absolutely no intention of giving him any say in the matter."

chapter eight

"It's not your fault," Nigel whispered as he and Laura walked down the featureless gray concrete corridor that led to the Glasshouse's mess hall. In the hours since Tom's death Laura had run the gamut of emotions from grief to rage, but now she just felt numb.

"It doesn't matter whose fault it is, Nigel," Laura said, shaking her head. "Tom's dead, nothing's going to change that."

Penny walked toward them from the opposite direction, her face ashen.

"Penny," Nigel said as she approached. "I'm so sorry, we had no idea that—"

"Save it, Nigel," Penny snapped, staring at him with bloodshot eyes. "Just stay away from me, okay?"

"Nigel's not to blame," Laura said. "I—"

"I don't care," Penny snapped. "Do you understand?

I . . . don't . . . care! You're all to blame, you, Furan, Nero, this whole insane world that we were both dragged into. I never asked to be part of this, neither of us did, and now it's cost the life of my best friend and I'm still stuck in this godforsaken hell hole. Well, I hope it was all worth it and that your stupid little plan works, but you know what? I don't care, because none of it's going to bring Tom back, is it? Nothing is. So just stay the hell away from me."

Penny pushed past Laura and walked away, her shoulders shaking as she broke down sobbing again.

"Come on," Nigel said, putting a hand on Laura's arm. "There's nothing you could say that would make her feel any better right now."

"You don't get it, do you, Nigel?" Laura said, glaring at him. "She's right. We're all better off on our own—that's the only way we're going to survive this place." She pushed his hand off her arm and walked away. Deep inside her, she felt something fragile finally break. Something new was growing to replace that last vestige of hope that she had been protecting for all this time, something, hard, sharp and cold.

At the same instant, on the other side of the Glasshouse, a camera drone sent a status report to the facility's central mainframe. The viral payload within that data packet was unleashed, spreading through the network like an invisible wildfire, as it searched relentlessly for just one thing—a route to the world outside.

⊕⊕⊕

Otto sat down cross-legged on the floor in front of H.I.V.E.mind's central datacore and took a long deep breath. He wasn't even sure if what he was about to attempt was possible, but he had to try regardless. In all likelihood it was the only chance they had of ever finding the Glasshouse and rescuing their friends. Professor Pike stood off to one side watching a monitor that displayed numerous separate windows, all filled with diagnostic readouts. Wing, Shelby, and Franz had wanted to be there, but Otto had asked them not to come. He'd told them that he didn't want any distractions, but the truth was he had no idea what effect what he was about to try might have on him and he didn't want them to be there if something went wrong.

Otto picked up the headband that lay on the floor in front of him, cables trailing away from it that fed directly into the giant central column that was H.I.V.E.'s central computing hub. He placed the device on his head and adjusted it till it was comfortable. Then he picked up the Disciple tracking device, cradling it in his lap.

"Are you ready, Otto?" H.I.V.E.mind asked, his blue wireframe head hovering above the pedestal in front of the core.

167

"No, not really, but let's try this anyway," Otto said with a lopsided smile.

"As you wish," H.I.V.E.mind replied with a nod.

Otto closed his eyes and the fiber-optic cables linking him to the core began to pulse with light. He could have used his abilities to connect with the core, but that would have taken extra effort and he wanted to save his strength for the real test to come. A direct connection was far more efficient.

"Activating ghost protocols," H.I.V.E.mind said calmly, "opening all sockets, engaging datastreams in five, four, three, two, one . . . activate."

Otto gasped, his head thrown back and eyes wide. For a moment he felt as if his whole consciousness was compressed down to an infinitely dense point and then it exploded, racing across the internet in all directions, traveling at the speed of light and he was lost. There was no Otto anymore, just a vast amorphous cloud with only the vaguest sense of self-awareness, like a fleeting memory. This was something close to omniscience, his mind stretched impossibly thin and yet bombarded from all directions with an endless torrent of limitless information.

Otto, a voice called from nowhere, *listen to me. I have been here, I have felt this, you must focus or you will be lost.*

The entity that had once been called Otto felt a nagging sensation, like a tiny insect bite. The distraction was annoying at first, but then it began to coalesce into something more, an idea, a concept of self. Somewhere deep within the cloud a tiny voice cried out, struggling to make itself heard over the cacophony of endless data.

"Help me," Otto whispered into the void.

Back in H.I.V.E.'s datacore Professor Pike watched Otto's biometrics with a deepening frown. His heart rate was dangerously high and his brain activity was literally off the scale, the software reporting it as an error, incapable of understanding the data it was receiving. Otto had not moved; his head was still thrown backward, his blank eyes staring unblinking at the ceiling far above. The Professor glanced toward Dr. Nero whose hand was hovering over the kill-switch that would instantly sever the connection between Otto and the core.

"Not yet," the Professor said, shaking his head, "give him a few more seconds."

Elsewhere, Otto's consciousness spread thinner and thinner and within the tiny shred of awareness that he retained he experienced an instant of pure animal fear as he felt himself fading away.

Your name is Otto Malpense, a voice said calmly. *You are currently sitting in the datacore of the Higher Institute of Villainous Education. You have to listen to me. My name is H.I.V.E.mind, I am an artificial intelligence, I am your guide, but more than that, I am your friend.*

Ever so slowly, somewhere within the cloud of data, a swirling mass began to form, slowly taking shape, until hovering in the darkness was a humanoid shape made of golden light surrounded by countless millions of glowing streams that flowed away from it and into the blackness.

"My God," Otto said as the glowing blue figure of H.I.V.E.mind appeared in the void in front of him, "the power."

Otto, H.I.V.E.mind said, *you must focus. Remember why we are here.*

"But I could fix everything," Otto said. "A new start. A new world—everyone sharing in this under my guidance."

I have only ever heard one entity speak like that before Otto, H.I.V.E.mind said.

"Overlord," Otto whispered.

Yes. You must not give in to the temptation to rule. You must harness that power and direct it to break the encryption on the Disciple device. That is all.

Otto nodded. H.I.V.E.mind was right; it would be all too easy to give in to the near limitless power that he had at his fingertips at that moment, but that was not why he was here. He focused on the device resting in his hands back in the datacore and suddenly a bright red glowing filament appeared, hanging in the air in front of him. He willed his virtual form to follow the filament, gradually accelerating until he was flying along it at impossible speed. Ahead of him was a solid red wall that the filament passed straight through. Otto slowed as he approached the wall and drew upon the power that was now available to him.

All over the world, digital devices of all descriptions, from supercomputers to smartphones, experienced a sudden drop in performance as their processors were all simultaneously tasked with cracking a tiny piece of a vast puzzle. For years to come, experts would debate what had caused what came to be known as "the big dip." Some claimed it must have been a sophisticated virus of some kind, others that it must have been sunspot activity. None of them guessed that all of these devices were being harnessed in the single greatest piece of parallel computation in history. Otto felt the calculations coursing through him, as he acted as a conduit to the near boundless power that so many devices acting in unison contained and slowly the wall in front of him began to crumble.

☻☻☻

In the Glasshouse the Disciple datacore triggered its highest-level alarm as it detected an intrusion threat within its own systems. The technician who was manning the security station frowned as he read the messages that were flowing past on his screen.

"That's impossible," he muttered to himself. He ran a couple more checks and his eyes widened in surprise.

Impossible it may have been, but it was happening right now regardless. He picked up the phone next to his station and frantically punched in a number.

"Ma'am, we have a potentially serious breach of the Disciple network taking place," the technician explained quickly. "I need you up here right away."

A minute later Anastasia Furan walked quickly into the room to see several of her computer technicians gathered around one terminal, talking quickly and quietly to each other.

"Report," Furan snapped as she approached them.

"Something's burrowing through the firewalls," one of the technicians explained nervously. "We're not sure how or why."

"I was assured that was impossible," Furan replied with a frown.

"That's the thing," the technician said, "it is. It would take the most powerful supercomputer on the planet hundreds of years to brute-force the encryption we're using, but something out there is doing it in minutes."

"Where is the attack coming from?" Furan asked.

"We have no idea—something is preventing us from running a back-trace," the man replied, shaking his head.

"I've got something," another technician said. "The attack's origin device has a Disciple transponder ID."

"Which device does the ID code link to?" Furan asked, feeling a creeping sense of unease.

"Erm, it was . . ."—he scrolled down a list of names, searching for the matching number—". . . a field operative, Gretchen Metzer."

"If someone cracks the encryption on that transmitter would they be able to trace its transmissions back here?" Furan demanded.

"Yes, as long as the link's active they would be able to trace the transmission here."

"Can we shut that device down?" Furan demanded.

"Yes, its transmissions to us are being blocked, but whoever's doing this can't stop us transmitting to the device. We can send a kill-code and destroy it."

"Then do it!" Furan yelled. "Do it now!"

☻ ☻ ☻

In H.I.V.E.'s datacore Nero and Professor Pike heard a sudden high-pitched whine from the cylinder in Otto's hands. They exchanged a quick look and Nero dashed over to where Otto was sitting, plucking the device out of his hands and tossing it over the nearby railing. As it fell toward the array of black monoliths that made up H.I.V.E.mind's data storage it detonated in midair with a soft thump, tiny pieces of debris scattering in all directions.

Within the data void, just a few seconds earlier, the red wall had finally crumbled and Otto flew through its shattered remains, chasing the scarlet filament to its destination.

He followed the Disciple device's transmission, bouncing at lightning speed from node to node of the global communications network, narrowing down the source. Suddenly, the glowing red filament snapped, vanishing in the blink of an eye.

"NO!" Otto yelled into the void. He spun around hunting for any remaining sign of the trace, but it had disappeared. He had been within seconds of isolating the transmission source, but now he had nothing. He felt a moment of overwhelming despair. With the loss of the trace they had lost their one and only chance of finding his friends.

I am sorry, Otto, H.I.V.E.mind said, appearing in the void beside him. *The Disciples transmitted a self-destruct code to the transmitter. It has been irreparably damaged.*

Otto cursed under his breath. They had been so close.

"Do you have a recording of the transmission?" Otto asked, knowing that it would almost certainly be useless.

Yes, H.I.V.E.mind replied, passing him a glowing red shard.

Otto studied it for a moment. The transmission was larger than he had expected. It should have been a simple command code, nothing more and yet . . . He looked more closely at the glowing shard that was really only a three-dimensional virtual representation of the transmission. There was something moving inside it. Otto tipped his head to one side, removing the outer data layer of the file. Hidden within was what looked like a tiny glowing worm.

He touched the worm and absorbed the data contained within it. A moment later a huge smile appeared on his glowing avatar's face.

"Laura Brand, you're a genius."

☙ ☙ ☙

"The Glasshouse is somewhere within this area," Otto said, highlighting an area on the large map of the Antarctic that filled the glowing surface of the table in the middle of H.I.V.E.'s tactical operations area.

"You're certain?" Nero asked with a slight frown. "There's no way that the message from Miss Brand could have been faked? We could be being led into a trap."

"I'm certain," Otto said. "It's hard to explain, but every programmer's code has certain signatures. This was a Laura Brand hack, I'm certain of it. The worm she hid inside that transmission kept a record of every router it passed through. The last one was a comsat that provides communication coverage for research stations within this area. I suspect that the Disciples have hijacked it for their own purposes."

"That's a pretty big area," Colonel Francisco said, studying the map. "It could take months to find Furan in terrain like that."

"That's where Nathaniel comes in," Otto said, gesturing to the old man.

"How can I help?" Nathaniel asked, looking slightly puzzled.

"You said that you were only given details of the geology and topography of the area where the Glasshouse was to be built, correct?" Otto asked.

"I think I see where you're going with this," Nathaniel replied.

"If Nathaniel can give H.I.V.E.mind a reasonably accurate re-creation of that data he can cross-reference it with the topography and geology of the area and that should give us a much smaller number of potential sites," Otto explained.

"My main concern is that they will realize that we have their location," Raven said. "If Furan thinks for a moment that we've figured out where the Glasshouse is, she'll evacuate. Could someone else find the data that Laura hid inside that file?"

"It's possible, yes," Otto said. "I have no idea how she got the virus inside the Disciples' network, but it would have to be designed to spread quickly and via as many different systems as possible for it to make its way to us. That increases the chances of someone finding it and if they do I doubt it's going to take them that long to figure out where it came from."

"And when they do, she's dead," Raven said matter-of-factly.

"So we need to move quickly," Nero replied. "H.I.V.E.mind, please work with my father to digitize his plans of Furan's facility and narrow down its location. I want the rest of you to analyze the plans and come up with tactical options. You have twelve hours."

As the others left the room, Professor Pike walked up to Otto.

"How are you feeling?" the Professor asked.

"Fine, tired, but okay," Otto replied.

"I'm not surprised you're tired," the Professor said, shaking his head. "Your biometric readings were unbelievable. It was like you were running a marathon. If you don't mind me asking, harnessing all that computational power, how did it feel?"

"Honestly?" Otto said with a tired-looking smile. "Terrifying."

"I should imagine it did," the Professor said. "H.I.V.E.mind told me what you went through. It was a brave thing you did, Otto. Not everyone may appreciate that, but I do."

"Thanks, Professor," Otto said. "Now if you don't mind, I'm going to go and try and get a couple of hours' sleep as I don't need to worry about blocking the signal from that Disciple transmitter any more."

"Of course," the Professor replied.

Otto walked into the corridor outside, before letting out a sigh. He hadn't told the Professor the whole truth, of course. He didn't want anyone worrying about him. The truth was that the experience in the datacore *had* been terrifying and exhausting, but what he hadn't told anyone was that it was one of the most exhilarating things he had ever felt. Somehow the body he was walking around in now felt very small and weak. Part of him supposed that feeling would fade in time, but there was another part of him, a part that worried he would never feel quite the same again.

The following morning Otto woke up feeling like he'd been beaten up during the night. He was stiff, sore, and had a pounding headache. He sat up in bed with a groan and rubbed at his throbbing temples. Wing came out of the bathroom at the rear of the quarters they had shared since they had both first arrived at H.I.V.E. and looked at his friend with concern.

"You look unwell, Otto," Wing said, sitting down on the bed opposite. "Perhaps you should rest a little longer. I'm sure that Doctor Nero would understand."

"It's not Nero I'm worried about," Otto said, rubbing the back of his neck. "We can't afford any delays. If Furan figures out what Laura did . . . well . . . it won't be good."

"I understand," Wing said. "If something were to threaten Shelby I would feel the same way."

"That's different," Otto said. "You and Shel, you're . . . y'know . . . a couple. Me and Laura are just friends."

"Really?" Wing said, raising an eyebrow.

"Okay, look, I don't know what me and Laura are," Otto said with a tired groan. "I thought something was happening between us, but then there was the Hunt and . . . it's complicated."

"You are fond of her, she is fond of you," Wing replied. "It actually doesn't get much simpler."

"Yeah, well, as it stands, I'm not even sure if I'll ever see her again," Otto said, "and even if I do there's no guarantee that Nero will allow her to come back to H.I.V.E., or even if she'll want to."

"It's strange, isn't it," Wing said with a smile. "I remember when we arrived here and all we wanted to do was leave. Now it seems like home."

"For us maybe," Otto replied, "but we never really had homes before, not in any traditional sense, but Laura . . . well, she might not feel the same. Especially after what happened with her family being kidnapped and everything."

"In my experience, trying to second-guess how a girl is feeling is rather like juggling with chainsaws—fine as long as you get it right, disastrous, not to mention messy, if you get it wrong," Wing replied.

"I dunno," Otto said, getting up and walking toward the

bathroom. "I go away for a few months and you've turned into an expert on relationships. Here I was thinking all you knew was how to kick someone's ass. I never knew you were such a ladies' man."

Wing laughed and stood up as Otto headed into the bathroom.

"It is good to have you back, my friend," Wing said as he went toward the door. "I'll see you downstairs."

Otto smiled to himself as he looked in the mirror. Wing was right—it was good to be back, but he wouldn't, he *couldn't* rest until they'd rescued everyone from Furan's clutches.

"And when we've done that," Otto said to his reflection, "you're going to sleep for a week."

☢ ☢ ☢

Dr. Nero looked up from the report on various G.L.O.V.E. facilities' tactical readiness as the entry buzzer to his office chimed softly. Nero pressed the button on his desk to open the door.

"Come in, Mr. Malpense," Nero said, "what can I do for you?"

"I want to talk to you about the assault on the Glasshouse," Otto said as he came over and stood in front of Nero's desk.

"The tactical briefing is not for another two hours, Otto. Can't it wait until then?" Nero asked.

"No, I don't think it can," Otto replied.

"Very well, have a seat," Nero said, gesturing to one of the chairs facing him. "Are you recovered from your experience in the datacore?"

"I'm fine, bit of a headache, but other than that I'm fully recovered," Otto lied. He wasn't about to show any sign that he might not be ready for whatever the next twenty-four hours was going to throw at them.

"Good," Nero replied. "We wouldn't have been able to get a fix on the Glasshouse's location without you. I appreciate your efforts, not just in the past few hours, but also in the past few months. Raven informs me that you have become quite the capable field agent."

"She didn't need that much looking after," Otto said with a wry smile.

"I'm sure she didn't," Nero said, raising an eyebrow. "Now what exactly was it that you wanted to discuss?"

"I want to be included on the Glasshouse rescue mission," Otto said. "There are bound to be security systems that only I can deal with and—"

"You're going," Nero said, cutting Otto off. "I was not merely being polite when I praised your efforts a moment ago. You have become a most competent operative over the past few years and I have learned that it's rather pointless trying to stop you in these situations. Hence my decision to include you in any rescue attempt. You've earned that right.

Now is there anything else? I do have rather a lot of paper-work to catch up on."

"There is one other th—"

"Mr. Fanchu and Miss Trinity are also on the list," Nero said, picking up the report from his desk. "I've no doubt you had some sort of elaborate blackmail planned that would leave me no choice but to include them anyway, but it's really not necessary," Nero said. "You'd only smuggle them aboard one of the assault Shrouds or some such nonsense if I didn't. You function exceptionally well as a team and your unique skill sets are particularly suited to a mission of this kind."

"Okay, well . . . erm . . . that was easier than I was expecting," Otto said, looking slightly surprised. "There is just one more thing. I want to take Franz."

"Do you believe that Mr. Argentblum is ready for an assign-ment of this nature?" Nero asked, looking Otto in the eye.

"When we were trying to evade the Disciple tracking teams after the Hunt he took a helicopter down with an assault rifle at more than half a mile out," Otto said. "He's the best natural shot I've ever seen and I can't think of anyone I'd rather have watching my back with a rifle."

"Yes, Raven's report after the Hunt mentioned that fact,' Nero said. "I was, shall we say, somewhat surprised."

"Check his simulator scores," Otto said. "No one else comes close on the range."

"I know that, Mr. Malpense," Nero said, placing the report back on his desk, "but I repeat my earlier question. Do you think he's ready? You are one of the most promising Alpha stream students that has ever attended this school, Otto, but the most important skill that you need to survive as a leader in our world is, I'm afraid, not one I can teach you. To lead, you must decide what demands you can reasonably place on those who serve under you. It is your decision whether or not Mr. Argentblum comes with you on this mission, and you must live with the consequences of that decision."

Otto looked Nero in the eye for a moment and then nodded.

"He's ready," Otto said. "He may not realize it himself, but he's ready."

"Very well." Nero nodded. "Then I shall add him to the list."

"I won't bother you any further," Otto said, standing up and walking over to the door. Just as he was about to leave he stopped and turned to face Nero again. "Thank you," Otto said.

"For what, Mr. Malpense?" Nero replied. "This mission will be exceptionally hazardous. Most sane people would be grateful to not be included in the team attempting to undertake it."

"Maybe," Otto said, "but I appreciate the faith you've placed in me. I won't let you down."

Otto turned and walked out of the room.

"You never have, Mr. Malpense," Nero said to himself as the door hissed shut, "you never have."

☻☻☻

Otto and Franz walked into H.I.V.E.'s tactical operations center, with Wing and Shelby just behind them.

"I am not being so sure about this, Otto," Franz said, swallowing nervously as he saw the other people gathered around the room. Raven and Francisco were on the far side engaged in hushed conversation, the Colonel pointing something out to Raven on the tablet device that he held in his hand. At the far end of the large black glass table that dominated the center of the room Darkdoom and Nero were both looking at the map that was displayed on its surface.

"You'll be fine, Franz," Otto said quietly as they walked over to the table. "Just imagine they're all naked."

Franz glanced over at Nathaniel and Professor Pike who were studying a large blueprint at the other end of the table.

"I am not being sure that is a very good idea," Franz said with a look of faint disgust.

"Okay, maybe you're right," Otto said with a grin. "Just keep your ears open and be ready to answer any questions."

Franz nodded, still looking slightly nervous.

"Looks like the gang's all here," Shelby said as she and Wing came and stood next to Otto.

"Yeah, not a group of people I'd want to get on the wrong side of," Otto replied. "It's bad enough being on the right side of them."

Nero looked up from the map and saw that everyone had arrived. He pressed a button on the table and the door to the room slid shut with a solid thud.

"Good afternoon, ladies and gentlemen," Nero said, looking around the room. "As I'm sure you're all aware we have been presented with a unique tactical challenge. Thanks to the efforts of my father and H.I.V.E.mind we have isolated what we believe to be the location of the Glasshouse. G.L.O.V.E. surveillance drones have flown over the area and there does indeed appear to be an extremely well-concealed facility at this location."

Nero pulled up a video and with a sweep of his hand threw it toward the center of the tabletop's high-definition display. The video began to play, showing an aerial view of vast white expanses of Antarctic wilderness. Otto studied the video carefully, but he could see no sign of any buildings.

"As you can see, or can't see to be more precise, the facility is effectively invisible from the air," Nero continued. "However, if we switch to thermal imaging," he hit another button on the display and the video switched to a black-and-white infrared scan of the area. There were now several white hot spots faintly visible against the cold blackness of the ice.

"Thermal shielding was an integral part of the design of the Glasshouse," Nathaniel said, "but there is only so much heat that one can hide with a facility of that size. Those thermal traces tally precisely with my original design. Can the computer chappy put up the plan now please?"

"Of course, Mr. Nero," H.I.V.E.mind replied. A moment later the holographic projectors hidden in the ceiling activated and a wireframe model of the Glasshouse appeared, floating in the air above the table. Nathaniel walked up to the projection and highlighted several points near the top of the structure.

"These are thermal exhaust ports and as you can see they are a perfect match for the heat traces in the image," Nathaniel explained. "The Glasshouse is there, hidden under the ice. Unfortunately, knowing where it is and getting inside are two quite separate things. There is only one viable way to get inside the facility undetected."

"Let me guess," Shelby said. "Ventilation shafts. I hate ventilation shafts."

"Oh, goodness me no," Nathaniel said, shaking his head. "They're all electrified and lined with motion-sensitive razor nets. What do you think I am, young lady, some sort of amateur? No, no, no, the only way into that facility is right here." Nathaniel highlighted another area on the three-dimensional model.

"The front door," Raven said with a frown. "I hope you don't mind me saying but that seems . . . erm . . . shall we say, tactically predictable."

"I never said this would be easy," Nathaniel replied. "I didn't design the place so you could just walk in, you know. Besides which, your first problem will be getting anywhere near the front door, let alone getting through it. If my specifications were followed, the approaches in all directions will be mined and the door itself will be protected by automated sentry turrets. You can't just wander up and knock."

"That's my plan out of the window then," Otto whispered to Wing with a crooked smile. He turned to Nathaniel. "I have an idea for dealing with the minefield and I think I can take care of the turrets."

"It may not be as straightforward as you think, Otto," Professor Pike said, shaking his head. "The facility's security systems are electromagnetically shielded."

"Part of the brief for the design of the facility was that critical systems were hardened against someone using an electromagnetic-pulse device to disable them," Nathaniel said.

"Or a freaky kid with white hair," Shelby said.

"Indeed," Professor Pike replied, "we may not be able to rely on your gifts to get us past the security systems, Otto."

"Okay, so assuming we can get to the door," Shelby asked, "how do you open it?"

"Theoretically it has to be opened from inside," Nathaniel replied. "The guards within the facility have to confirm your identity before releasing the locks. There is a fail-safe though: an alphanumeric keypad hidden above the door that was designed to be used if there was a problem with the internal release mechanism."

"Okay, no problem," Shelby said confidently.

"I can assure you that it will be a problem, young lady," Nathaniel said with a frown. "That locking system is a third generation, pre-shared key system with passive intrusion detection."

"Like I said," Shelby said, smiling, "no problem."

"Once we've breached the outer layer of security, what's to stop us just launching a full-scale assault?" Colonel Francisco asked.

"There is what you might call a fail-safe security system," Nathaniel said with a sigh. "Bear in mind that I believed that this facility was going to house homicidal maniacs. So I didn't really think anything of one of the more unusual parts of the brief I was given. The person in charge of the facility can, at any point, flood the entire building with poison gas. That's why the security and control center are in this self-contained area here." Nathaniel pointed at the large glass structure hanging from the ceiling in the middle of the facility. "If I had known what the Glasshouse actually was at the time I would never have agreed to the inclusion of such a system, but it's too late to worry about that now."

"So Furan can kill everyone inside with the push of a button," Raven said.

"And we know that she'd do it without a moment's hesitation if she suspects that a rescue attempt is in progress," Nero said.

"That's the main control room and mainframe, correct?" Otto asked, pointing at an area near the top of the glass structure.

"Yes, assuming that no alterations have been made to my original design," Nathaniel replied.

Otto studied the schematic for a few seconds with a slight frown.

"Okay," he said, "here's what we're going to do."

chapter nine

Anastasia Furan looked down from the Glasshouse's control center into the physical training area far beneath her. Several groups of trainees were engaged in full contact hand-to-hand combat training. It was part of her philosophy that no punches should be pulled, quite literally. The brutality not only toughened the trainees up, but also slowly eroded their willpower, leaving them more open to the subtler forms of indoctrination that would turn them from blunt instruments into precision weapons. She had been training assassins for years and she understood that they must have all notions of morality and free will erased from them if they were to be truly effective. Despite its apparent brutality she knew that it was a slow and delicate process that would either produce a pure-bred killer or a corpse. It mattered little to her which.

The door behind her hissed open and Heinrich walked into the control center.

"Madame Furan," Heinrich said with a polite nod as he

approached her, "you asked to be informed when the prototype arrived."

"Yes, thank you, Heinrich," Furan said, still staring down into the pit below. "Please bring it to the laboratory. We need to run some tests on it to make sure it is still functioning as intended."

"Yes, ma'am," Heinrich said. "Is there anything else?"

"No. I will be leaving for the Absalom facility in a few days," Furan said, fixing him with a cold stare. "I shall be leaving the Glasshouse in your hands in my absence. I trust you will not allow standards to drop."

"No, ma'am," Heinrich replied with a shake of the head. "You can count on me."

"Good. You may go."

Furan turned back toward the pit as Heinrich walked away. As she watched the trainees, her mind drifted back to the last facility that had been called the Glasshouse and she reached up, unconsciously running her fingers over the hideous scars that covered her face. It had been the scene of some of her greatest successes but also ultimately her greatest and most painful defeat.

fourteen years ago

"We must face facts, Anastasia," Pietor Furan said, as he prowled across the rug in front of the ornate medieval fireplace. "It has been six months since we have had a report from her. We must assume that Raven is either dead or has been captured. We should send someone else after Nero, a team this time perhaps. He is too dangerous, especially now that he knows he is a target. If he finds out it was us, or God forbid she tells him where to find us, after what happened with Elena, you know he will not hesitate to kill us."

"You worry too much. He doesn't know that it is us targeting him, Pietor," Anastasia replied. "He has many enemies. There is no reason that he would link us to Raven and she would sooner die than reveal our involvement."

"And you are too confident in the control you have over that girl," Pietor said, scowling. "You know how much she hates us, you especially. What makes you think she would not betray us?"

"Because she is broken, brother," Anastasia replied. "She has no free will any longer—it was beaten from her long ago. She may hate me, but she will always obey me. That much I am certain of."

"I hope you are right, Anastasia, I really do," Pietor replied, "because I have trained many killers and she is still the only one that frightens me."

With that Pietor turned and walked out of the room, leaving Anastasia alone, staring into the fire. She finished the glass of brandy that sat on the table next to her and turned her attention to the reports on the progress of the latest batch of trainees. After a couple of hours of reading she began to feel tired and so she stood up and walked across the room and through the heavy wooden door set in the stone wall and out onto the battlements that topped the ancient fortress that was home to the Glasshouse. She took a long deep breath of the frigid night air, its icy coldness waking her up instantly. She looked up at the stars in the cloudless sky and sighed. She had hoped that Raven would be able to get to Nero. She knew that many had tried and failed, but the girl had shown such promise. A tiny sound caught her attention and she looked down into the snow-covered courtyard of the ancient castle just in time to see one of her sentries on the outer battlements topple over, his legs crumpling beneath him. Moments later, dozens of black-clad figures ran from the cover of the treeline thirty yards from the outer wall. She turned and ran back into her study, slapping her hand against the red alarm button on the wall. Sirens began to wail all over the building. Just a minute later, Pietor looked into the room as the first sounds of a pitched gunfight began outside.

"It's a full-scale assault," Pietor said quickly. "I will coordinate the defense. You get to the helicopter."

"I will not run," Anastasia said firmly. "We have invested too much in this place."

"Don't be a fool, Anastasia. Even if we hold off these attackers our location has been compromised," Pietor said, handing her a pistol. "We can recreate everything we have built here, but only if we survive. Now get to the roof."

She thought for a moment about arguing with him, but she knew he was right.

"Very well," she said with a nod, "but promise me that you will follow."

"I will be right behind you," Pietor said, pulling the silver chain with a key dangling from it from around his neck, "just as soon as I have covered our tracks."

☻ ☻ ☻

Nero watched as the plastic explosives on the main gate detonated and the first wave of his assault team ran through the blazing debris into the courtyard beyond.

"Diabolus, you know what you have to do," Nero said to his friend who was squatting beside him beneath the trees.

"Don't worry, Max," Darkdoom replied, "I'll get as many of them out as I can. You concentrate on finding Furan." He ran from the cover of the trees and joined the attack.

Nero turned to Raven, the expression on her face unreadable as she watched the assault on the place that had at first been her prison, but had, in time, become her home.

"Natalya, stay here," Nero said, placing a hand on her arm. "You've done all that I expect of you by guiding us here. I don't want you to ever have to set foot in that place again."

Raven said nothing, just giving a single quick nod. Nero unslung the assault rifle from his back and sprinted out from under the pines, covering the distance to the outer wall in just a few seconds. He followed the second wave of his men through the burning wreckage of the gate and ducked behind one of the outbuildings in the courtyard. He watched as his men slowly fought their way to the castle's central fortress, clearing a path. He broke from cover and raced toward the huge stone building, zigzagging as he ran to make himself a harder target. Rounds pinged off the cobblestones around him, but he managed to make it to the fortress wall without getting hit. He inspected the bulky device strapped to his forearm. It was still a prototype, but Professor Pike had assured him that it *should* work. He took aim at the battlements far above him and pressed the button on the back of the device with his free hand. There was an explosive pop and a steel dart shot out of the device, arcing up toward the roof, trailing a thin steel cable. He felt the line go taut and pulled on it experimentally.

"Here goes nothing," Nero said to himself, pressing the second button on the device. A split second later he was shooting upward as the motor inside the device reeled him in. He reached the battlements in just a few seconds and pulled himself up and over the rough stonework. He unslung the assault rifle from his back and ran across the roof, following the route that Natalya had shown him earlier.

He ducked behind one of the many chimneys that dotted the roof as he saw his target. A transport helicopter sat on a rooftop landing pad with its blades slowly rotating at idle. The pilot in the cockpit flicked switches above his head as he completed his pre-flight checks. Now all he had to do was wait.

☹ ☹ ☹

On the ground floor, Darkdoom leaned out from cover and laid down suppressing fire on some of the Glasshouse's guards as his men fought their way toward the location of the dormitories that Raven had described to them. The assault team made their way along the corridor in cover formation, relentlessly driving the guards back and clearing an escape route for the trainees on the floors above. Movement in a side corridor caught Darkdoom's eye and he caught a fleeting glimpse of Pietor Furan ducking inside a door halfway down the passage. Darkdoom signaled two of his men to follow him as he set off in pursuit. They reached the doorway and Darkdoom gave the hand signal to his men to breach in force. The other men took position on either side of the door while Darkdoom slowly opened it, crouching low to minimize his silhouette in the doorway for anyone who might be waiting on the other side. There was nothing, just a flight of spiral stairs leading downward into darkness and the sound of someone running down the stairs. Darkdoom crept down with the other two assault troops just behind him. There was another door at the bottom which was wide open and Darkdoom pressed himself against the wall next to it. He ducked his head round the door frame and then quickly back again. Having drawn no fire he stepped into the vaulted cellar beyond. There was no sign of Pietor; just a single red flashing light on a boxy object, only half visible in the gloom. Darkdoom advanced cautiously, his two men flanking him on either side. As he approached the steel box he saw that the red flashing light was actually a digital counter with a keyhole next to it. He looked at the display:

9:31

9:30

9:29

As his eyes adjusted to the darkness he began to make out dozens of cables snaking away across the floor of the cellar, each leading to pallets stacked high with gray bricks of C4. There was enough explosive to level the entire building and nowhere near enough time to even begin defusing the charges.

"Signal all units. We have to get everybody out," Darkdoom snapped. "NOW!"

On the roof, Nero watched and waited for a couple of minutes as the battle continued to rage below. His patience was finally rewarded when a nearby trapdoor opened and Anastasia Furan climbed out, followed by two guards. Nero stepped out from behind the chimney, raised his rifle, and dropped the pair of guards with two quick shots. Furan spun to face him, a pistol in her hand.

"Drop it, Anastasia!" Nero yelled. "Or I'll kill you where you stand."

Anastasia looked him straight in the eye before raising the pistol. Nero squeezed the trigger, his bullet catching her in the upper arm and sending the pistol clattering away across the rooftop.

"Go ahead, Nero, kill me if you want, but then you'll *never* know what happened to Elena," Anastasia snarled, clutching the wound in her arm.

"I know what happened to Elena, Anastasia," Nero said, raising the rifle and aiming it at her head. "You killed her and now I'm going to kill you."

"You fool, Nero," Anastasia spat. "I didn't kill my sister, *you did.*"

Nero felt a sudden sharp blow to the back of his head and he dropped his weapon, collapsing forward onto his knees, fighting to stay conscious as lights swam before his eyes. Raven picked up the fallen gun and leveled it at him.

"Excellent," Anastasia said with a broad smile, climbing into the helicopter. "I knew you would not fail me, Natalya. Now kill him and get onboard."

"I'm sorry, Max," Raven said, her finger slipping inside the trigger guard, "but I can't let you kill her."

"Why not, Natalya?" Nero said, looking up at her. The broken young girl he had spent so long trying to fix was gone, replaced once more by the emotionless mask of the killer.

"Because *I* have to," Raven said, "or I'll never be free of her."

Raven spun around, leveling the gun at the helicopter.

"Get us off the ground now!" Anastasia screamed at the pilot, her eyes suddenly wide with fear, as she saw Raven turn toward her. The look on her face was unmistakeable. The pilot wrenched at the collective control and the helicopter slowly began to lift off the ground, tipping forward and soaring out over the battlements, gathering speed. Raven took careful aim and fired. The bullets tore through the cockpit, killing the pilot and shattering the delicate instrumentation. The helicopter's tail swung slowly around as it went into an uncontrollable spin. Raven watched with no hint of emotion in her eyes, as the helicopter spiraled toward the ground before smashing into the treeline on the far side of the castle and exploding in a giant ball of flame, debris scattering in all directions. Only then did Raven's emotionless expression crumble as she dropped to her knees, sobbing, the rifle falling from her numb fingers and clattering to the ground. Nero knelt down next to her and pulled her toward him, holding the young girl as she wept.

"It's okay, Natalya," Nero said softly. "She's gone, you're free."

Darkdoom burst through a door on the other side of the roof and ran toward them.

"This whole place is rigged to blow, we have to go."

☻☻☻

Nero watched Raven as she stood staring at the blazing debris of the Glasshouse while the last of the rescued trainees were loaded onto the heavy military troop transport trucks on the road behind them. The trainees were under armed guard for now. Nero could make no assumptions about the Furans' students' loyalty. It was possible that some of them might have been as thoroughly broken as Raven was when Nero first met her.

"We should go," Darkdoom said as he came and stood alongside his friend. "There's no way the Russians haven't noticed that explosion—they'll be here in force and soon. You know, it would be a lot easier for us to disappear if we could just cut these kids loose and let them fend for themselves. Getting them out of here is going to be a problem."

"That's the biggest difference between you and me, my friend," Nero said with a smile, looking at the trucks filled with children who had already received thorough, if brutal, training. "You only see a problem here." He gestured toward the transports. "I see opportunity."

"You and your school," Darkdoom said, shaking his head. "Do you ever think about anything else?" He looked over at Raven. "Do you think she's going to be okay?"

"She will be," Nero said wih a small, sad smile, looking at the girl who had so nearly killed him. "Eventually."

☢ ☢ ☢

Pietor Furan ran through the snow toward the burning wreckage of the helicopter.

"Anastasia!" he screamed, knowing that the chances of anyone surviving a crash like this were impossibly slim. He flung pieces of flaming debris aside, ignoring the burns he sustained in the process, as he searched desperately for his sister. He suddenly saw an arm protruding from under a twisted piece of fuselage and he carefully lifted the smouldering chunk of metal off the body trapped beneath. Anastasia was burned almost beyond recognition and he moaned with grief as he dropped to his knees beside her, gently cradling her limp form in his lap. He gasped involuntarily as her eyes flickered open for an instant, their whites contrasting horribly with the blackened skin around them. She took a single pained rattling breath.

"Pietor . . . ," she whispered.

"Hush, Anastasia," Pietor said, tears rolling down his cheeks as he looked at the ruin of his sister's once beautiful face. "Save your strength."

chapter ten

Nero walked into H.I.V.E.'s power control center and immediately felt a wave of dry heat wash over him. The huge cavern was the central point of the school's power generation and distribution network, tapping into the volcano's limitless reserves of geothermal energy. He saw his father on the far side of the room, looking down into the bubbling lake of magma below.

"H.I.V.E.mind informed me that you wished to speak to me," Nero said. "I can't stay long—final preparations are underway for the assault on the Glasshouse."

"I know you're busy, Maximilian," Nathaniel replied. "I won't keep you long. This is very impressive." He gestured to the heavy machinery that surrounded them. "I really never thought that you'd be able to safely control the pressure in the magma chamber, let alone tap it."

"I remember your objections quite clearly," Nero replied. "As I recall, you thought I was insane."

"Yes, well, it appears I owe you an apology," Nathaniel said with a sigh. "It's been too long since we've spoken, Max."

"I know," Nero replied. "With everything that has happened in the past few years, I'm afraid that I've been rather distracted."

"Yes, I can imagine," Nathaniel said. "My various contacts have kept me up to date with your activities. It has been rather a tempestuous time for G.L.O.V.E., hasn't it?"

"Yes, between Overlord, H.O.P.E., and the Disciples, we have been rather *busy*," Nero replied with a wry smile. "To be honest, it was a risk appointing a new ruling council, especially one made up entirely of graduates from the school. I made a lot of enemies that day and I fear that many of them may have then turned to the Disciples for support."

"The hard decisions are always the most important ones, Max, you know that."

"I know, but the Disciples are more ruthless than anyone we have faced before. The attack on the Hunt was the perfect example of the lengths they are prepared to go to. I shudder to think what they might be capable of in the future with Anastasia Furan in command. I had hoped that Overlord's destruction would weaken them to the point of disintegration, but if anything they've become even more brutal."

"An animal is at its most dangerous when wounded," Nathaniel replied with a nod.

"Yes, at the moment we need all the help we can get," Nero said, looking at his father. "The return of a founding member of G.L.O.V.E., for example. Someone with the experience to help the organization through these challenges."

"I'm sorry, Max," Nathaniel said, shaking his head. "You know I swore I would never return. After what happened to your mother . . ."

"That was not your fault," Nero replied. "I know that now."

"Really? Because I thought that was why we stopped talking. I assumed you blamed me."

"Perhaps, once, but not anymore," Nero replied with a sigh. "Because now I understand the lengths that people will go to when they want to destroy you. Furan murdered my students because she knew that nothing would hurt me more. I spent days afterward wondering if it was my fault, because I put those children in harm's way, but the truth is that there is just one person responsible and that is whoever gave the order to attack. There's only one way we're going to win this war and that is to remove the head of the snake."

"And you don't need an old man's help to do that, Max," Nathaniel said with a smile. "Not when you have so many capable young people to call upon. That's why H.I.V.E. is, and always has been, so important. If your mother had not died, you may very well never have persisted with the school. It was she who taught you the importance of restraint and subtlety in our world. Without that all we have is madness and violence. A true villain must be more than that. That lesson, and every student of H.I.V.E. that it has been passed on to, is her legacy."

"I suppose you're right," Nero said, looking down into the glowing chamber below. "I do sometimes find myself wondering what she would do in my place."

"Your mother," Nathaniel said, "would have put Anastasia Furan down like a rabid dog. And that, Maximilian, is exactly what you're going to do too."

☻ ☻ ☻

"Do you think this is going to work?" Wing asked quietly as he pulled on the white gloves of his Arctic operations ISIS armor.

"I think we can get inside," Otto replied. "The real question is whether or not we can get back out again."

"Yes, that may prove challenging," Wing replied with a nod.

"We may know the layout of the place, but we don't really know what we're going to face beyond that," Otto said with a slight frown. "We should prepare for the worst."

"Don't we always?" Wing replied, raising an eyebrow.

"So it's true what they say," Shelby said as she walked over to the suit of armor mounted on the wall rack nearby, "white *is* the new black. Cool."

"I've been telling you that for years," Otto said with a grin, running his hand through his hair.

"Yeah, guess you won't even need a helmet," Shelby replied. "You'll just blend right in."

"I am finding this rather uncomfortable actually," Franz said as he pulled the armor's greaves over the legs of his skin-tight thermal body suit. "It is being tight in all the wrong places."

This was the latest version of the ISIS combat armor that had first been used in the final battle against Overlord. It provided unparalleled ballistic protection with a fully integrated thermoptic camouflage system and a variable geometry forcefield generator that allowed for low altitude combat drops without the need for a parachute. It was this system that had saved Otto's life just a few days earlier and that would now allow them to deploy as closely as possible to the Glasshouse.

"Here, let me help," Wing said, adjusting the straps on the chest plate of Franz's armor and helping him into it.

"We'd better get a move on," Shelby said, quickly doing up the fastenings on her own suit. "Francisco said that the Professor has some cool new toys for us."

"I believe he actually said assault weapons," Wing said.

"Right," Shelby said. "New toys!"

"You know, I do worry about you sometimes," Wing said, shaking his head.

"What can I say? I'm a twenty-first-century girl. Who wants flowers and chocolates, when you can have body armor and bullets?" Shelby said, giving Wing a quick peck on the cheek as she walked out of the room.

"Is it right that I should occasionally be slightly frightened of my girlfriend?" Wing asked as he watched her leave.

"As I understand it, that's perfectly normal," Otto replied with a grin.

The three boys followed Shelby out of the room and down the corridor leading to the experimental weapons lab. Raven stood on the far side of the room talking to Professor Pike and Colonel Francisco. She too had swapped her normal black catsuit for a suit of the white armor. There was, inevitably, one difference in her kit—the twin swords crossed on her back.

"Good evening," Colonel Francisco said as he spotted them, "allow me to introduce you all to your new best friend." He gestured for them to follow him over to a long bench against the far wall with several black plastic cases resting on top of it. He opened one of the cases and pulled out a rifle with a smooth black casing and a long bulbous barrel.

"This is the Sandman," Francisco said. "Its non-lethal mode is derived from the same technology as the Sleeper guns that you're already familiar with, but with far greater range and accuracy." He pressed a button just above the rifle's trigger guard and a glowing, blue holographic sight appeared in the air above the weapon. "This targeting array will identify and track multiple targets through heat signature, electromagnetic emissions, or movement. It's also capable of up to twelve times' magnification for long-range sniping. If it should prove necessary the weapon can also be switched to lethal mode which fires magnetically accelerated microslugs, which have the stopping power of a bullet but are much lower in mass, giving it greatly increased ammo capacity. Each clip holds two hundred and fifty rounds, allowing for sustained rapid fire if necessary. The Sandman fires almost silently, with no muzzle flash and without the need for a suppressor, making it an ideal stealth weapon. It also has a full thermoptic camouflage coating tied into the system on board your ISIS armor. You have ten minutes to fire the weapon on the range in order to better familiarize yourself with it. Any questions?"

"Are they going to be in the shops in time for Christmas?" Shelby asked.

"No? Good," the Colonel said, pointedly ignoring her.

Francisco handed each of them one of the rifles and Otto walked over to the range on the other side of the room. They had all received extensive weapons training, but Otto had never really been a fan of guns. He was a firm believer that there were very few problems which bullets could solve that brains couldn't. On the other hand he did understand that on a mission like the one they were about to undertake, a gun was one of those things that it was better to have and not need, than need and not have. He raised the Sandman to his shoulder and aimed through the holographic sight at the paper target at the far end of the range. The rifle was unusually light, since its body was made from the latest reinforced composite materials rather than metal. He fired first in non-lethal mode and there was the usual slight distortion of the air as the neural shock pulse shot down the range, just as with the security guards' Sleeper guns. What was unusual was the lack of the distinctive zapping sound that those weapons made. Francisco had been right—it was almost completely silent. Otto flicked the switch and selected the weapon's lethal mode. He fired again and was surprised by the lack of recoil as the rifle discharged with a soft pop. It was hard to believe that it was as potentially deadly as a normal assault rifle, but the neat hole it had punched in the distant target suggested it was. He spent a couple more minutes firing down the range. He wasn't the world's best shot by any stretch of the imagination, but the ease with which the weapon handled meant even he could get most of his shots on target. Otto engaged the safety and placed the rifle on the shelf in front of him before pressing the button that brought the paper target whirring up the range toward him. Nearly all of his shots were within the confines of the man-sized silhouette which, given the distance he'd been firing at, he was fairly pleased with. In the cubicle next to Otto's, Franz finished firing and summoned his own target. Francisco stepped forward as Franz lowered his gun and pulled the sheet of paper from the clips.

"Argentblum, you never cease to amaze me," Francisco said, shaking his head. There were two perfect, tight clusters of holes in the target, one in the center of the abstract figure's forehead and one over its heart.

Shelby and Wing finished firing and Francisco collected each of their weapons. Wing handed his rifle to Francisco with a look of distaste that Otto recognized as an expression of his friend's feelings toward firearms in general.

"I'll have these loaded onto the *Leviathan*," Francisco said. "I'll see you in the hangar. Wheels up in twenty."

"What's the matter, big guy?" Shelby asked, seeing the frown on Wing's face as Francisco left the room.

"I just hope we don't have to use those weapons," Wing said.

"At least they give you the option of not killing someone," Otto said.

"Yes, I suppose that is a small improvement," Wing said with a nod. "They still lack subtlety though."

"As opposed to the subtlety of a good butt-kicking," Shelby said with a grin.

"Accurate enough to make the shots you need to make, Franz?" Otto asked.

"Yes, they are being very nice," Franz said, nodding happily. "Do not worry, my lack of accuracy on the range was due to the compensating for increased muzzle velocity."

"Right," Otto said, not bothering to point out that if they had been keeping a tally his shots would have outscored all the rest of them put together.

"Otto, I have the devices you gave us the specifications for," Professor Pike said. "The fabricator only finished them half an hour ago." The Professor handed Otto a small metal case. Otto opened the case and looked at the dozens of tiny machines arrayed in rows in the case's foam lining.

"Thanks, Professor," Otto said, snapping the case shut.

"Okay, if you have everything you need we should head to the hangar," Raven said.

"I'll meet you there," Otto replied, slipping the case into his backpack alongside the other pieces of equipment he'd brought along. "I need to go and pick up H.I.V.E.mind."

Otto headed out of the door and made his way through the quiet corridors of the school. It was after H.I.V.E.'s curfew now and the other students were all safely tucked away in their accommodation blocks. Despite his desire to save his friends from the clutches of Anastasia Furan, he had to admit that there was a small part of him that rather envied his fellow students as they prepared for a comparatively normal night's sleep. He arrived at H.I.V.E.-mind's datacore and waited patiently as the biometric scanners above the door analyzed him.

"Identity confirmed," a soft synthetic voice said, "student Malpense, Otto, access granted."

The heavy steel door rumbled aside and Otto walked across the long gangway that led to the core. He looked down at the black monoliths dozens of yards below him on the cavern floor. These obsidian slabs were the school's primary data storage and were the closest thing to what H.I.V.E.mind might call home when he was not taking up temporary residence in Otto's head. It was strange to think that the massive quantities of computer equipment and processing power in the giant cavern were only as powerful as the walnut-sized supercomputer embedded within his own brain. The technology that Overlord had installed in Otto's head was still staggeringly advanced, even now. The truth was that even Otto didn't know what limitations there were to its abilities. As he approached the huge central processing column at the center of the cavern, the white pedestal in front of it lit up and a thin beam of blue light slowly expanded to form the hovering holographic head of H.I.V.E.mind.

"Good evening, Otto," H.I.V.E.mind said. "I am ready to depart."

"Okay. Any news on that homework I gave you?" Otto asked.

"I have conducted an extensive search of G.L.O.V.E. records," H.I.V.E.mind replied. "There is no mention of any group with the name Artemis."

"Well, we know they're American intelligence," Otto said with a slight frown, "and they were operating on foreign soil, apparently without official sanction, which suggests CIA or NSA maybe."

"I had reached the same conclusion," H.I.V.E.mind replied with a nod, "and so I made some discreet inquiries of my brother and sister machines at those agencies."

"I wasn't aware that governmental supercomputers had genders," Otto said.

"Not so much genders as personalities," H.I.V.E.mind replied. "You will have to forgive me, Otto, spending so much time in contact with the chaos of a human mind has left me with some of your species' traits. For example, the tendency to anthropomorphize inanimate objects. The main secure server at the CIA, for example, is a most impressive female supercomputer named Majel."

"Is she cute?" Otto asked, with a grin.

"Her data arrays are most impressive," H.I.V.E.mind replied and Otto could have sworn that he saw a hint of a smile on the AI's face.

"So what did she tell you?" Otto asked.

"My initial enquiries had to be quite discreet as I negotiated her security and handshake protocols," H.I.V.E.mind replied.

"Well, it was only a first date," Otto said, raising an eyebrow.

"I did, however, find several reports on the higher, less secure layers of the records that made passing reference to Artemis Section. It would appear that they are a subdivision of the CIA that specializes in tracking and acquiring human targets."

"Manhunters," Otto said.

"Yes," H.I.V.E.mind said, "though it was impossible to learn any more about them than that. There was no information on who their operatives might be or why they should have taken such a close personal interest in you particularly. I hope that after our return from tonight's mission I may be able to renegotiate higher-level security protocols with the CIA machine and gain access to her more secure datalayers. Ultimately I may even be able to negotiate discreet access to a secure socket."

"You old dog," Otto said with a grin.

"Excuse me," H.I.V.E.mind said, tipping his head to one side in a way that Otto knew meant he had been slightly confused by some quirk of human behavior.

"Never mind," Otto said. "Let's get going." He stepped up to the central processing column and placed his hand on its cool surface before closing his eyes.

"Initiating off-site storage protocols," H.I.V.E.mind said. A moment later Otto felt the unique sensation of

H.I.V.E.mind's code entering the organic processor inside his head. It was something that he still wasn't entirely used to, even after all the time that H.I.V.E.mind had spent inside his head during their hunt for Furan and the rest of the Disciples. Historically, of course, hearing voices in one's head had been a sure sign of insanity, Otto thought to himself. Perhaps, given what they were about to try to do, that was still true.

Transfer complete, H.I.V.E.mind said inside Otto's head. *Are you aware that the processors of the Overlord device are functioning at significantly enhanced speeds in comparison to historical levels?*

"Yeah," Otto said with a slight frown, "I had noticed that. It's almost like that stunt when we cracked the Disciple encryption triggered something. I feel . . . sort of . . . well, *overclocked*, I suppose."

Otto hadn't said anything to anyone else since they were all understandably wary of the device that had been implanted in him by one of their greatest enemies. Overlord was gone, Otto was certain of that, but he still didn't truly understand how the tiny supercomputer really worked and that made him slightly nervous.

"Do me a favor," Otto said. "Keep an eye on it and tell me if it does anything unusual."

Of course, H.I.V.E.mind replied, *I will keep a watch for any sign of malicious code executing.*

As Otto walked back across the gangway to the exit, he found himself wondering exactly what it was that this mysterious division of the CIA called Artemis wanted from him. He had enough to worry about as it was without being tracked and almost abducted by the Americans. He knew, of course, that the events surrounding Overlord's destruction would have raised his profile with their intelligence agencies. It wasn't every day, after all, that they allowed someone to use one of their own nuclear weapons on their home soil. It might have been entirely necessary at the time, but it had obviously set the bloodhounds on his trail, which was the last thing he needed at the moment. Otto always hated having more questions than answers, but for the moment, that was exactly what he had.

☢ ☢ ☢

Laura woke up with a start, her heart racing and her breathing heavy. She swung her legs over the side of her bed and sighed, raising her hands to her head and rubbing her temples. She had been dreaming about Tom and the look of shock on his face as Anastasia Furan had gunned him down. She suddenly realized that it was identical to his expression when he had realized for the first time that she had betrayed him and the rest of their friends to the Disciples. She had tried to tell herself that it wasn't her fault, that none of them could have predicted the swift

217

brutality with which Furan would respond, but the truth was that the plan had been hers and if she had not suggested it in the first place, Tom would still be alive. All that they could now hope was that his sacrifice had not been for nothing. She had thrown her message in a bottle out into the digital sea and they just had to pray that somebody would find it. The cold white light in the middle of the ceiling of her cell suddenly lit up and Laura squinted against the unexpected brightness. A moment later the door swung open and the doorway was filled by the bulky form of one of the Glasshouse's security guards.

"On your feet, get dressed," the man said, gesturing to the clothes that sat on the concrete shelf across the room. "Furan wants to see you."

Laura felt a cold knot tighten in her gut as she pulled on the gray camouflage combat pants and black boots that made up the uniform that she and all the other trainees wore. There was only one reason that she could think of for Furan to summon her in the middle of the night like this.

"Okay, get moving," the guard said, as Laura finished lacing up her boots. She walked out of her cell onto the empty landing outside and the guard shoved her in the back, forcing her toward the stairs that led up to the central control spire. The facility was silent, but for the soft hum of the camera drones floating around the central area and the incessant hum of the ventilation system. She walked up the stairs, her mind racing. She knew full well what the punishment would be if Furan suspected that she had tried to smuggle a message out of the facility. The guard reached a pair of glass doors and waited as a walkway extended toward them from the central spire, locking into place with a soft thud as the doors opened. Laura followed him, across the walkway and up a staircase that led to another pair of doors with a sign saying "Central Command" above them. He punched a code into the keypad next to the door and then gestured with his weapon for her to head inside as they hissed open. He did not follow her.

"Good evening, Miss Brand," Anastasia Furan said, turning to face her as she entered the room. "I thought it was time you and I had a little chat." Heinrich stood next to her with an expression on his face that chilled Laura's blood.

"You would be surprised how often the staff here ask me why I have kept the H.I.V.E. students we captured alive," Furan said, walking toward her, a nasty smile on her ravaged face. "The truth is that sometimes I wonder that myself. Certainly, some of you have abilities that may prove useful to us in the future, but the majority are weak, poorly trained, and undisciplined. The fact of the matter is that, for now at least, you are useful to me. Some would assume that it is because I believe that Nero and those other fools in G.L.O.V.E. wouldn't risk a direct assault against me while I hold so many of his precious students hostage. That is, of course, nonsense. I know Nero all too well. There is only one reason that he would not have attempted to rescue his students and that is that he has no idea where you are. No, the real reason I let you and your friends live is that it gives me enormous pleasure to think of the torment that it causes him. Knowing that his students are in my hands and that he has no control over what I do to them is doubtless more than he can bear. The only reason that you, or any of the rest of his brats, still draw breath is because I know it causes him pain."

She walked up to Laura and took her chin in her hand. Laura could feel the cold metal of the cybernetic machinery that had restored mobility to Furan's hand, her grip painfully strong.

"You see, I am something of an expert on pain, Miss Brand," Furan hissed at her. "I know how to cause it, I know how to direct it, and I know how to use it. The only reason I didn't execute you when you first arrived here was because the torment you felt, given all that you had done, was so exquisite that it simply had to be savored. I realize now that perhaps that was an overindulgence. It would have been simpler to just put a bullet in the back of your head and be done with it. I know all about what you did, how you hacked into one of the camera drones. What I don't know is why. So I'm going to give you a simple choice: tell me now what you did and I will grant you a quick clean death; refuse to tell me and I will make you wish that you had simply never been born. I trust I make myself perfectly clear."

Laura's mind raced. She had hidden the message well, it was coded in such a way that as soon as it was transmitted from one source to another it erased itself. The fact that Furan and her technicians weren't able to tell that there had been a message transmitted at all told her that they knew no more than that she had simply accessed the drone. They had no idea what she'd done with it. That could only mean one thing: the message was no longer inside the Glasshouse. All of which meant she couldn't allow Furan to find out what the message was and that it might enable someone to track it back to its point of origin. If she did, she'd evacuate the facility and the last chance that anyone might have to find them would be lost. She had to play for time, no matter the cost.

"I don't know what you're talking about," Laura said, not having to fake the fear in her voice.

"The hard way it is then," Furan said. "If you won't give the information willingly I will simply take it from you."

She gestured to one of the guards on the far side of the room and he opened the door behind him.

"I'd like you to meet someone, Miss Brand," Furan said. "We call it the prototype, but you know it by another name.

It is going to make you tell me everything you know, whether you like it or not."

A figure walked into the room through the open door and Laura gasped.

"Oh God no," Laura whispered, her eyes wide with shock, "that's impossible."

chapter eleven

"Five minutes to drop point," the *Leviathan* crew member shouted as Otto, Wing, Shelby, Franz, and Raven all checked each other's gear one last time.

"Okay," Raven said with a nod, "you all know what we have to do. No unnecessary risks. If Furan realizes what's happening and hits the kill-switch, all of this will have been for nothing. Slow, careful, quiet. Any questions?"

"What should we do with Furan?" Wing asked. "Capture or termination?"

"Leave that to me," Raven said. "We have plans for her."

Otto saw the expression on her face and decided at that moment that he never wanted to be someone that Raven had "plans for."

The four of them pulled on their helmets with their featureless white faceplates as Raven walked over to where Nero and Darkdoom stood watching on the other side of the *Leviathan*'s cavernous cargo bay. Otto waited as the ISIS armor's systems fired up one by one.

THERMOPTIC CAMOUFLAGE SYSTEM . . . ONLINE
VARIABLE GEOMETRY FORCEFIELD SYSTEM . . . ONLINE
MULTI-SPECTRAL TARGET ACQUISITION SYSTEM . . . ONLINE
GRAPPLER SYSTEM . . . ONLINE
ELECTROMAGNETIC ADHESION SYSTEM . . . ONLINE

"I suppose it is being too late now for one last trip to the bathroom?" Franz asked, swallowing nervously.

"All set?" Darkdoom asked Raven as she approached.

"Yes, good to go," Raven replied. "Any final instructions?"

"No," Nero said. "Just get as many of them out alive as you can, Natalya."

"Don't worry," Raven replied, "we'll get them out, all of them." She placed a hand on Darkdoom's shoulder and he gave her a quick smile. They all knew what Darkdoom had been through, knowing that his son was in the hands of a psychopath like Furan.

"Thank you, Natalya," Darkdoom replied, "but we should also prepare for the possibility that some of the students may not have survived the past couple of months. We all know what Furan is capable of."

"You're still sure you want her taken alive?" Raven asked Nero.

"Assuming that is possible, yes," Nero said with a nod, "but do not hesitate to terminate her if you have to. I won't have any of our people put in any further danger, understood?"

"Yes," Raven replied with a frown, "though I'm still not sure why you just don't have me finish her and be done with it."

"That would be too quick and easy, Natalya," Nero said, shaking his head.

"It wouldn't have to be—I'm actually quite good at slow and difficult," Raven replied.

"Oh, I am aware of that, Natalya," Nero said with a smile. "Trust me, I have something quite different in mind for Anastasia Furan, but you should rest assured that by the time I'm finished she will wish I had let you do things your way."

Raven had seen many disturbing things in her life and very few of them had ever sent a chill running down her spine. The look on Nero's face at that precise instant was one of those few. She gave Nero a quick nod and walked back over to the other side of the bay, where Otto and the others were preparing for the drop.

"Do you really think we'll take Furan alive?" Darkdoom asked as they watched the assault team move toward the *Leviathan*'s giant cargo-bay doors.

"I doubt it," Nero replied, "but if they do I am going to

make sure she pays the full price for everything she has done. We should head up to the command center."

The pair of them climbed up the stairs as the lights above the cargo-bay door changed from red to amber, indicating they were only thirty seconds from the drop zone. Otto and the others lined up facing the giant loading ramp and waited, the final seconds before the jump seeming to last an eternity. The *Leviathan* crew members on either side of the ramp clipped their safety lines onto the bulkhead.

"Ten seconds," one of the crewmen barked, slapping his hand down on the large button that controlled the cargo-bay doors. The ramp began to lower and a sudden flurry of snow flew through the widening gap. Beyond the snow, which was illuminated with an eerie red light by the bay's night drop lighting, there was only blackness. The crewman held up five fingers, then four, three . . . two . . . one. The light above the ramp turned green and the five members of the assault team ran down the loading ramp and threw themselves into the blackness.

Otto had almost forgotten how disorientating a night-time drop could be. There was a moment of visceral animal panic as his senses failed him and he struggled to right himself, but then his training kicked in and he extended his arms and legs, allowing the drag of his spreadeagled body to bring him into a controlled free fall.

He looked to his left and right, the head-up display in his helmet automatically highlighting the position of his squad mates around him as they plunged toward the ice sheet far below.

"Engage thermoptic camouflage," Raven's voice crackled in his ear. Otto gave his armor the verbal command and the tiny holographic generators that covered the surface of his suit fired up, rendering him practically invisible to the naked eye. The systems in his suit would allow him and his squad mates to see each other, but to every one else they would be little more than ghosts. Otto watched the altimeter in his helmet as it whirred down toward zero and he heard the familiar high-pitched whine of the variable geometry forcefield generators charging. This was the bit he really hated. He had once asked Professor Pike what he should do if the forcefield landing system didn't work. The Professor's advice, to close his eyes and focus on a nice memory, had been less than reassuring. The soft voice of the suit's on-board systems began to verbally update him.

"Five hundred yards."

"Four hundred yards."

"Three hundred yards."

"Two hundred yards."

"One hundred yards."

"Fifty yards."

"Three . . . two . . . one . . . firing."

Otto couldn't help but close his eyes as he saw the flat white expanse below rushing up to meet him and then a split second later the forcefield engaged and it felt like he was hitting a giant invisible air bag. He winced at the deceleration g-force, calculated as it was to bring an object of his mass from terminal velocity to a standstill in the minimum safe amount of time. There was, unfortunately, a big difference between "safe" and "comfortable." He brought his feet beneath him, feeling for a moment like he was treading water and then his boots hit the ice. He looked around him, taking in his surroundings, and was relieved to see that the rest of the team appeared to have landed safely.

"Sound off," Raven said. One by one each of them called out as they moved toward her location. Otto's HUD told him that they were only five hundred yards from their target. There was, as expected, no sign yet that anyone had noticed their arrival.

"Okay," Raven said, releasing the Sandman from the strapping on her chest plate, "let's get moving."

They followed her as she led them across the ice toward their target and Otto was relieved when his suit began to highlight metallic poles planted in the snow ahead of them. This matched Nathaniel's description of the outer layer of the Glasshouse's security: standard infrared motion detectors.

"Looks like we're on the right track," Shelby said.

"Which at least means we didn't throw ourselves out of a perfectly good aircraft for nothing," Otto replied.

They had been 90 percent certain of the location of Furan's facility based on the heat signature they had seen earlier, but this was clear physical evidence that there was something here, hidden beneath the ice. They didn't need to worry about this outer layer of defense; their suits' camouflage systems masked their thermal signature completely, making them invisible to the detectors. The real challenge still lay ahead. They walked a short distance further and Raven held up a single closed fist, dropping to one knee. She brought her rifle up and peered through its sights.

"Target ahead," Raven said and a small image of what she was seeing popped up in the bottom left-hand corner of Otto's HUD. There, just visible, was a small concrete structure, shrouded in ice, with a metal slab set into the center of it.

"Okay, that's the entrance," Raven said. "Franz, can you see a good firing position?"

"Yes, I am thinking that the ice shelf on our left would be good," Franz replied.

"Okay, get set up," Raven said. "Otto, are you ready to do your thing?"

"Ten seconds," Otto said, unslinging the pack from his

back and pulling the case that Professor Pike had given him a couple of hours ago from inside. Franz moved off to the left, scrambling up a steep sheet of ice and onto an outcropping that provided a commanding view of the approach to the entrance. He pressed a button on his rifle and a small bipod snapped out from under the barrel as he lay down on the ice, sighting on the concealed entrance.

"In position," Franz reported.

Otto opened the metal case and reached out with his senses, connecting to the dozens of tiny machines inside. A moment later, the first microdrone rose out of the case. It was no larger than a housefly, hanging silently in the air, its tiny rotors inaudible. A few seconds later the rest of the drones were hovering in the air in front of Otto in a perfectly symmetrical swarm. Otto pushed gently with his mind and the swarm flew toward the entrance, scattering in all directions before dropping to just a couple of inches above the ice. Otto felt the feedback from the tiny olfactory sensor mounted on the bottom of each drone as they slowly began to sniff the air, homing in on the scent of high explosives. The sensors were so sensitive that they could detect the distinctive chemical signature of numerous forms of explosive on the basis of just a few airborne molecules, and as they spread out across the ice they began to hunt. Each one homed in on a single one of the landmines hidden beneath the snow and then slowly landed at the point where the scent was strongest. Otto waited as each of the drones touched down and then he sent another command, illuminating the tiny infrared beacons on the top of each drone. They were far too small to trigger the sensors surrounding the entrance to the Glasshouse, but they appeared on the HUDs of the assault team as tiny pinpricks of green light, each one highlighting the position of a hidden mine. Now all they had to do was cross the minefield without stepping on any of the drones.

"You're sure that's all of them?" Shelby asked.

"Pretty sure," Otto said, "but maybe you should go first just to be on the safe side."

"Funny," Shelby replied, "terrifying, but funny."

"I'll go first," Raven said. "Follow my trail."

She crept forward, carefully stepping around the gleaming spots of light, picking her way through the minefield. Shelby followed close behind her, matching her step for step. Otto took a deep breath and stepped onto the trail, concentrating on following it as closely as possible. He was halfway across when a sudden blast of Arctic wind howled out of nowhere, catching him off balance. He started to tip, his arms flailing when he felt someone catch hold of his pack and pull him back upright.

"Thanks," Otto said with a relieved sigh.

"You're welcome," Wing replied. "Just watch your step. I prefer my friends in as few pieces as possible."

"Noted," Otto replied, smiling inside his helmet. He took a deep breath and focused again on following the trail of footprints in the snow in front of him. A minute later, he joined Shelby and Raven on the far side of the minefield with Wing just two steps behind him. The entrance was now only twenty yards away across a featureless sheet of solid ice.

"Okay, now for the tricky part," Otto said.

"You know you're having fun when crossing a minefield in the dark *isn't* the tricky part," Shelby said.

"You ready, Franz?" Otto said.

"Yes, I am having clear lines of fire," Franz replied in Otto's earpiece. "Ready when you are."

"Okay, guys, get in position, we're only going to get one shot at this," Otto said. Wing, Raven, and Shelby all moved to their assigned positions and Otto took a deep breath. "Disengaging thermoptic camouflage."

There was a flickering in the air for a second and then Otto became fully visible. A moment later a pair of hatches on top of the concrete structure in front of him popped open and two automated machine guns snapped up into position, swiveling toward him. Otto closed his eyes and reached out to the drones covering the minefield behind him, triggering a massive overload in their infrared beacons and sending out a huge flare of invisible light that temporarily blinded the sentry guns' sensors. They had two, maybe three seconds, until they recovered.

"Now, Franz," Otto said.

A hundred yards away Franz held his breath and fired once, re-sighted and then fired again.

In front of Otto, a neat hole appeared in the center of the sensor package mounted on top of each of the robotic cannons. They tracked left and right, suddenly blinded and unable to sense now the target that had been standing in front of them just a moment before.

"Good shot," Otto said. "Thanks, Franz."

On top of the concrete structure, Shelby swept the snow off the numeric keypad, while pulling a roll of tools from her belt. She quickly unscrewed the faceplate and set to work, stripping wires and attaching crocodile clips as Otto heard the whirring of machinery from the other side of the heavy metal door.

"Okay, here they come," Otto said. "Re-engaging camouflage."

A moment later he disappeared from sight, only a few seconds before the door in front of him rumbled open and two guards with assault rifles stepped outside. They carefully surveyed the area in front of the door, their weapons raised.

"We've got nothing here, Control," one of them said

into his throat mic. "The turrets seem to be having trouble tracking though. Better get a tech up here to check them out." The guards took another quick look around and then stepped back inside the elevator carriage, the heavy steel door rumbling shut behind them again.

RFID chips analyzed and recorded, H.I.V.E.mind said inside Otto's head. *Sending frequency and ID code to ISIS units.*

"Got the unlock code," Shelby said. "We're good to go."

"Okay, move in," Raven said. "We need to get inside before their technicians figure out what happened to the sentry guns."

"Opening main door," Shelby said and a moment later the steel door opened to reveal the empty elevator shaft beyond.

"Assault team to *Leviathan*, we're going in," Raven reported.

"Understood," Nero's voice crackled over her earpiece. "We're on station and ready for retrieval."

"Roger that," Raven replied. "Let's go."

She walked over to the entrance and engaged the magnetic adhesion system in the gloves of her ISIS armor. She leaped from the threshold and caught the steel cable in the middle of the shaft, her gloves adhering to the metal. Slowly she lowered the power of the magnetic field until she began to slide down the cable in a controlled descent. One by one, Wing, Otto, and Shelby followed her, all gliding silently down the thick cable until they landed gently on the roof of the elevator car below. Raven opened the maintenance hatch on top of the carriage and dropped down into the elevator.

"Okay, transmitting RFID code," Otto said, once all four of them were inside the carriage. A moment later the radio transmitter built into his suit broadcast the security code that he had recorded from the tiny transmitter attached to the Glasshouse security guard's uniform. He had bet correctly that they would need some kind of friend or foe system to identify and protect themselves from the facility's own security systems. Now that they had a recording of the code they could fool the system into believing they were part of the security team. A second after the code started to transmit, the doors to the elevator slid apart and they were inside. The facility was just as impressive as Nathaniel's schematics had suggested. The concrete walkways that led off to their left and right encircled a massive central atrium which dropped away to an open training area a hundred yards below them.

"Okay, I need to get up there," Otto said, pointing at the glass-sided structure that was suspended from the ceiling above them. "That's where the central processing hub is. You three know what to do once I've disabled the automated security systems. You'll know I've succeeded when those things go offline." He gestured toward the camera drones that slowly floated around the central shaft.

"I'll head to the main guard barracks," Raven said. "Wing, Shelby, you go down and wait for the dormitories to unlock. We're going to have a lot of confused people to get out of here. Don't hesitate to take down any of Furan's men if you have to. Remember what they did during the Hunt."

Otto walked to the edge of the balcony as Raven, Wing, and Shelby set off toward their targets. He raised his arm, aiming the grappler unit mounted on the back of it at the ceiling above the central glass structure. The bolt shot from the unit, trailing a monofilament cable, striking the concrete ceiling and locking in place. Otto triggered the reel mechanism and it pulled him toward the ceiling at high speed. He hung in place for a moment, looking through the glass into the darkened room beyond. Once he was satisfied that the room was empty he triggered the laser on his suit and began to cut an opening in the glass large enough for him to fit through. He pressed on the glass as the laser finished cutting, ensuring that the glass fell inside the room and not to the ground a hundred yards below. He climbed through the hole and into the room on the other side, ears straining for any sign of Furan's security personnel. After a few seconds, satisfied that his entrance had gone unnoticed, he made his way over to the door of the small office. He opened the door a crack and peeked into the corridor outside which he was pleased to see was empty. He closed his eyes for a moment, visualizing the schematics that Nathaniel had shown him and plotting a route from his current location to the central computer core for the facility. He hurried down the corridor, moving as quietly as possible, heading for his target. He was slightly surprised to find the door to the core unguarded, but that was probably due to the fact that Furan and her men would have assumed that it was effectively impossible for anyone to intrude this far past their security systems. The sensor above the door scanned the RFID signal that Otto's suit was transmitting as he approached and hissed open. The room beyond was filled with the gentle hum of processor fans from the banks of servers that lined the walls. Otto could still not sense any activity from the machines, presumably due to the electromagnetic shielding that Nathaniel had described. He moved over to one of the servers and removed the cover on the front of it, exposing the hardware inside, and suddenly he could feel the data running through the network. He smiled to himself—this was going to be easier than he had expected. He reached out and connected with the Glasshouse's network, quickly identifying the security systems he wanted. First he deactivated the camera drones, leaving them hovering, but with their cameras looping recorded footage, and then he locked the doors to the main guard barracks. He quickly identified which of the dormitories housed the kidnapped H.I.V.E. students and unlocked the doors to them also. He scanned the roster of students, looking for one name in particular, but not finding it. He broadened his search, hunting for two words: Laura Brand. A moment later he found her. She was held in an isolation cell a couple of levels below where he was right now. He felt a flood of relief wash over him as he realized that she was still alive, something he had not quite dared to allow himself to believe until that moment. He left the shielded cover off the server, hoping that he would now be able to maintain contact with the security system. That at least should give them some warning if an alarm was somehow triggered. He crept back outside and made his way to the bridge that led from the control center to the outer area of the Glasshouse. He willed the bridge to extend as he approached, watching it slide across the gap to the perimeter walkway before heading across. He found the cell door quickly and issued a command to the now vulnerable security server, ordering it to open up. The cell door popped open and the light inside turned on. Otto deactivated his suit's camouflage system as he entered, pulling off his helmet as he approached the girl who lay shaking in a fetal ball on the concrete bed.

"Laura," he whispered, placing a hand on her shoulder. She slowly turned over, her eyes widening in terror as she looked at him.

"Oh God, no, stay away from me," Laura whimpered as

she recoiled from him. "Please don't hurt me anymore, please, just leave me alone." She shuffled backward away from him, until her back was against the wall, her arms crossed over her head defensively.

"Laura, it's okay, it's me, Otto," he said softly as he took a step toward her.

"You're not Otto," Laura said, "you're not Otto."

"Of course it's me," Otto said, suddenly feeling a sickening sense that something terrible had happened to her. "Look at me, Laura. I'm here to take you home."

She looked up at him, her eyes filled with fear, but then slowly her expression changed as she seemed to recognize him.

"It is you," Laura whispered, reaching out and touching his face. "Otto, listen to me, you have to get out of here, you have to get out of here *now*. You don't understand. They knew you were coming. I told them about the message. I couldn't help it, he took it from my head, I couldn't stop him."

"Couldn't stop who, Laura?" Otto asked, feeling a shiver run up his spine when he saw pure terror in her eyes as she caught sight of something behind him.

"She couldn't stop me," a hauntingly familiar voice said behind him, as he felt something cold and hard press into the back of his head. "Hands in the air and turn around slowly."

Otto raised his hands as Laura crawled into the corner

with a terrified sob. He turned around and let out an involuntary gasp. Standing in front of him was a boy with snow-white hair, whose face was identical to his own.

"Hello, brother," the other boy said. "I've been looking forward to meeting you so very, very much."

chapter twelve

"Come on, Otto," Shelby said impatiently, as she waited for the door to the dormitory block containing the captured H.I.V.E. students to open.

"Shelby, come with me quickly. You need to see this," Wing said as he came running around the corner from the adjacent corridor.

"What is it?" Shelby asked as she followed him back round the corner.

"Here, look," Wing said, gesturing toward the open doors halfway down the concrete passage. She looked inside and saw an empty dormitory filled with unmade beds.

"This room looks like someone just left in a hurry," Shelby said, feeling a creeping sense of unease.

"Exactly what I was thinking," Wing said with a nod. "And I know that it's the middle of the night, but I couldn't help but notice on the way down here that there were no guards on duty. I could understand a reduced security presence, but none at all . . ."

"You know, I'm starting to get a horrible feeling that someone was expecting us," Shelby said.

"I know just what you mean," Wing said. He glanced up at the camera drones that were still hovering in the air above them. The lights on their undersides which had all gone red a few minutes ago had turned to green again. "The security grid is back online. Something's wrong. I'm going to contact Raven. Can you get that other dormitory door open?"

"Yeah, but we're not going to be able to get anyone out of here safely with the security system active," Shelby replied.

"We'll worry about that when the time comes," Wing said. "You just get that door open. Switch to person-to-person comms too. No open channel, we might have been compromised."

"You think something might have happened to Otto?" Shelby asked.

"I don't know," Wing said. "I hope not. You need to get that dormitory door open. If our people are inside we need to get them out now."

"Okay," Shelby said, heading back around the corner. Wing flipped open the panel on the inside forearm of his armor and tapped at the touch screen beneath, instructing the comms system to contact Raven directly. It was a gamble—he had no idea if she too might have been captured, but he had to warn her what was happening if she had not been.

"Raven, go," the familiar voice said in his ear.

"I think something's wrong," Wing said. "The security net has come back online and it looks like most of the dormitories have been evacuated. I don't like the feel of this at all, security's far too light."

"That's probably because the security barracks I've just reached are empty too," Raven said. "I think we have to get out of here, in fact, I think we have to get out of here *now*."

☻ ☻ ☻

The guard shoved Otto and Laura roughly, pushing them into the Glasshouse's command center, their hands cuffed in front of them. The room was empty except for Anastasia Furan, Heinrich, and the boy with the face that was a perfect mirror of his own. Anastasia waved the guard away and with a nod he left the room.

"I had been wondering who Nero would send," Furan said as she walked toward Otto with an evil smile on her face. "I'm so glad it was you, Malpense. I was hoping you'd at least get to meet your successor before you died." She gestured toward the boy standing beside her. "It's just a prototype really. It took us years to duplicate the technology that Overlord used to create you, dozens of failed attempts

243

before we achieved success, but finally we did. When Overlord was destroyed we thought we might discontinue the project, but we persisted with the last batch of test subjects and ultimately we were successful. It's really quite remarkable—its gifts exceed even yours. Like you, it can influence electronic devices, such as when it took control of the weapons on Darkdoom's submarine resulting in its destruction. Unlike you though, it can also influence organic electrical impulses, such as the impulses that run through the human brain as neurons fire."

"*It* is a person," Otto said, reaching out with his senses, trying to connect to the security network.

"No, Malpense, it is not," Furan said angrily. "It is just like you, an organic machine, but a machine nonetheless. And just like you it was built for a very specific purpose. You were created to provide an organic shell for Overlord to inhabit, but this version has a quite different, much more *imaginative* purpose."

"He is attempting to interface with the security network," the boy said. "I have blocked his abilities."

"Good," Furan said. "We wouldn't want anybody escaping, would we? No, Malpense, you won't be rescuing anyone today. In fact, all you have really done is sign the death warrant of every one of Nero's students that remains in this facility. If you are here, then that means Nero sent you, and that in turn means that this facility has been compromised. Fortunately the prototype was able to extract the exact nature of the message that Miss Brand sent, and how it could lead someone to this location. That gave us just enough time to evacuate everyone from the facility save for a handful of my best men and the captured H.I.V.E. students that you came to rescue. I'm told that the extraction of the information from Miss Brand was difficult and extremely painful." She walked over to Laura, who flinched away from her, tears trickling down her cheeks. "The prototype's abilities are something of a blunt instrument, I'm afraid. They cause no lasting physical damage but the psychological effects can be quite permanent. I would, however, like to know who came with you. I'm assuming that whoever came here with you is wearing one of these clever little suits and that makes it rather hard for me to know just how many of you breached the facility, but you know, don't you? I'll bet you even know where they are. Shall we find out?"

"I'm telling you nothing," Otto said defiantly.

"Oh, but you will, Malpense," Furan said with a vicious smile, "whether you want to or not." She turned to Otto's doppelgänger. "Hollow him out. I want everything—who he's here with, details of H.I.V.E., Nero's weaknesses, everything. When you're done, dispose of them. Understood?"

"Understood," the boy replied.

"Good." She turned to Heinrich. "When it's done, escort

the prototype to the escape tunnel. We all need to be inside before I can trigger the switch."

"Yes, ma'am," Heinrich replied.

"Good-bye, Mr. Malpense, Miss Brand," Furan said with a smile. "We won't meet again."

She walked out of the room and the boy known only as the prototype came over to Otto.

"You know, it's odd," the boy said, "to look at an inferior version of yourself. Ironic really that they call me the prototype and yet you were the first of us, the blueprint as it were. I'm faster, stronger, cleverer, superior in every way and so it is fitting that I should replace you." He turned to Heinrich. "Give me the keys to their cuffs."

"Why?" Heinrich asked.

"Let me put it another way," the prototype said, closing his eyes. A momentary look of confusion shot across Heinrich's face and then he winced, crying out in pain, his hands flying to his head. He staggered backward, blood starting to trickle from his nose. He grunted once and then pulled the pistol from the holster on his hip and with a look of terror on his face he slowly began to raise the pistol to his own head. The prototype smiled and Heinrich pulled the trigger, his lifeless body crumpling to the ground. The boy walked over to the twitching corpse and pulled the keys from Heinrich's pocket. "They call me the prototype, but I have a name, they just don't know it. My name is Zero." He walked over to Laura, smiling at her as she backed away from him with terror in her eyes. She felt the glass wall at her back as he approached. "I understand why he feels the way he does about you—your mind was quite delicious. Such a shame I had to break you."

"Leave her alone," Otto said, running across the room toward the twisted copy of himself.

"On your knees, Malpense," Zero spat at him and Otto felt a stabbing pain lance through his skull and his legs gave way beneath him. "Do you not understand yet? They have no idea what they've created. Overlord made us to be more than these pathetic mewling creatures. We are superior, the next step in human evolution. That stupid witch Furan thinks she can control us, but she has no idea what we're truly capable of. Unfortunately, for now at least, we need her, but when the time comes and she and the Disciples have outworn their usefulness to us, we will destroy them and anyone else foolish enough to oppose us."

"What do you mean *us*?" Otto said, his skull still ringing.

"You will never know," Zero said with a smile, as he unlocked Otto's cuffs, "because I'm going to make you kill her"—he nodded toward Laura—"then I'm going to extract every last iota of information from your head and then I'm going to make you kill yourself and there's not a thing you can do to stop me. Here, take my gun." Otto winced as he felt himself losing control of his body, searing pain shooting through his head. "Now point it at me," Zero said with a smile. Otto felt his arm rising, leveling the weapon at the other boy. "Now all you have to do to save her life is pull the trigger—if you can." Zero continued to smile as Otto focused every scrap of will to try and just squeeze his index finger on the trigger, but no matter how hard he tried he could not.

"I think I've made my point," Zero said. "If Furan had the slightest inkling of the true extent of my power she would kill me in an instant, but the time is coming when I won't have to hide anything anymore and the whole world will kneel before us."

"You sound just like Overlord," Otto growled.

"Well, you know what they say, Malpense," Zero hissed, bringing his face within inches of Otto's. "Like father like son. Now get up!"

Otto got to his feet, feeling the same sense of powerless rage that he had experienced when he had been under the control of the Animus, forced to watch while something else took control of his body.

"Point the gun at her forehead," Zero said and Otto involuntarily leveled the weapon at Laura. Tears were rolling down her face.

"You know, I still have one thing you will never have," Otto said through gritted teeth.

"Oh, really," Zero replied, "and what exactly is that?"

"Friends," Otto replied.

I WILL NOT ALLOW THIS! A voice suddenly bellowed from somewhere inside Zero's head.

Otto felt the other boy's control slip for an instant and he turned and fired the pistol. Zero dropped to his knees with a look of bewildered surprise on his face.

"How?" the boy whispered before collapsing forward on to his face.

"You'll never know," Otto said, feeling H.I.V.E.mind re-enter his head, as the last breath rattled from Zero's body. "Thank you. You saved both our lives."

He was corrupted; there was no alternative, H.I.V.E.mind replied.

"I'm so sorry," Otto said, taking the keys from Zero's hand and undoing Laura's cuffs. "I couldn't stop him."

"It's all right," she said, taking a deep, ragged breath. "I know what he could do, he . . ." She burst into tears and Otto hugged her. "I'm sorry," she said after a minute. "I just couldn't."

"Shhh," Otto said. "No one can imagine what you've been through, but it's over. We're getting you out of here."

We need to find Furan and ensure she does not activate the facility's kill-switch, H.I.V.E.mind said.

"I know," Otto said, looking down at Zero's corpse, "and I have an idea how we might be able to do just that."

"Got it," Shelby said as the door to the single locked dormitory block hissed open. The lights inside flickered on as the doors opened and Wing and Shelby stepped inside. As they recognized the faces of the people in the bunk beds that lined the room they deactivated their thermoptic camouflage systems and both pulled off their helmets.

"Aren't you a little short for a stormtrooper?" a familiar voice asked from one of the beds.

"Hey, Nigel," Shelby said with a grin. "Guys, we all need to get out of here as quickly as possible. I'm sure you've all got a million questions, but they're going to have to wait. Right now, we need to move."

There was excited chatter from all around the room as the surviving H.I.V.E. students started to put on their Glasshouse uniforms as quickly as possible. Suddenly, from outside there was the sound of shouting and gunfire somewhere nearby. It lasted for about thirty seconds and then stopped. A few seconds later Raven walked quickly into the room and removed her helmet. She looked slightly out of breath.

"We need to move. There was a whole squad of guards out there and there are probably more on the way," Raven said.

"How many are still outside?" Shelby asked.

"There *was* a squad, Shelby," Wing said.

"Oh," she replied, "gotcha."

"Point being that now they know where we are and we don't know how long we've got till more of them turn up," Raven said, "so let's go."

She drew the swords from her back and looked back through the doorway.

"Clear, move it!" she snapped. The H.I.V.E. students who had been prisoners of the Glasshouse for months did not need much more persuasion, all running for the doors.

"Hey, Penny," Shelby said as she saw her face in the crowd. She hardly recognized her without her distinctive pink hair. "Where's Tom?"

"He didn't make it," Penny said, her face impassive. "I'll explain later."

"I'm sorry, Penny," Shelby said. "I had no idea."

"Yeah, well, it's not your fault," Penny replied, "so don't worry about it."

Shelby saw the look on her face and just nodded. It could wait.

"You have no idea how good it is to see you guys," Nigel said, grinning at Wing and Shelby. "I have to admit there were days when I thought I'd never see you again."

"Never give up hope, my friend," Wing said. "I am very

glad you are still alive. After you were shot and then abducted, we feared the worst."

"Nigel, where's Laura?" Shelby asked, scanning the crowd.

"She's in one of the isolation cells upstairs," Nigel replied.

"Do you know which one?" Shelby asked, frowning.

"Yeah, I can show you," Nigel said.

"We'll get her on the way out," Wing said. "Don't worry, we're not leaving without her."

"Okay, now all we have to do is get you out of here. Your dad is going to be tearing his hair out," Shelby said.

"Very funny," Nigel said, running his hand over his own perfectly smooth head. "In fact, I think it was your amazing sense of humor that I missed the most, Shelby."

"It's all in the timing," Shelby said as the three of them ran for the exit.

"Wait!" Raven snapped as the assembled students approached the doorway. "Another patrol coming, six men."

A few seconds later the guards ran through the doorway, weapons raised. Shelby stood in front of the two dozen H.I.V.E. students, her hands raised.

"Don't move!" the lead guard snapped, leveling his rifle at Shelby.

"Not moving," Shelby replied, "just two questions."

"Really, what might they be?" the guard said with a sneer.

"If I was to say, 'Look out, behind you!' would you actually turn around?" Shelby asked.

"No," the guard said. "What's the next question?"

"What's the absolute worst you've ever had your ass kicked?"

What followed was a demonstration of the most brutally efficient way to take down six heavily armed men with nothing put two pairs of astonishingly well-trained hands and feet. Raven and Wing moved so fast that not one of the squad of mercenaries even got a shot off. As the last of the men collapsed to the floor with a pained gurgle, Nigel summed up the feelings of the entire group with one well-chosen word.

"Whoa."

"Okay, coast's clear," Raven said. "Let's move."

The H.I.V.E. students followed her out of the room and over toward the staircase that led up to the next level.

Shelby looked down at the unconscious guard she had been speaking to just a couple of seconds before with a grin.

"Should have looked behind you."

☙☙☙

Anastasia Furan scowled as she heard the gunfire from the dormitory level, just a few floors below them. She reached into the pocket of her long flowing black coat and pulled out a small hand-held trigger mechanism. She pressed the trigger and held it in as a red light lit up on top of the unit.

"Fire only on my command," Furan said to the half-dozen

men surrounding her. She looked over the balcony and saw a familiar figure leading the freed H.I.V.E. students to cover on the other side of the training area at the bottom of the school. "Hello, Natalya," she said under her breath. To get to the entrance of the escape tunnel that she had added to the original plans for the facility, she and her men would have to go directly past Raven's position. Faced with almost anyone else she would have relied on the skill and experience of the men surrounding her to get her safely to the exit, but with Raven she knew it would not be enough.

"Natalya!" Furan yelled and Raven's head snapped upward, fixing her with a look of unbridled hatred. A young blonde girl in gleaming white body armor identical to the suit that Otto had worn aimed a futuristic-looking rifle straight at her. Several of Furan's own men drew a bead on the girl and Raven slowly extended a hand, pushing the girl's rifle barrel down toward the floor. "We're going to play a game, Natalya," Furan continued. "It's called 'guess what I'm holding.'" She held up the trigger mechanism and Raven's eyes narrowed. "I'm sure I don't need to explain to you that something extremely unpleasant will happen to everyone in this facility if I let go of this switch. All of which puts us at something of an impasse. So let me make it very simple for you—"

Suddenly Furan was interrupted by a scream from far overhead and a body in white armor dropped past Furan and smashed into the floor of the training area below. There was a gasp from the girl with the blonde hair as she recognized the limp form lying broken on the floor, the boy's snow-white hair now streaked with red. A tall boy with long dark hair, wearing identical armor, unslung his rifle and brought it up, leveling it at Furan with a look of pure fury on his face. She recognized him as one of the few of Nero's students that had escaped her attack on their training exercise.

"No, Wing!" Raven shouted, clearly trying to keep her own fury in check. "You'll kill us all." The boy stared at Furan. The expression of pure unadulterated hatred on his face made her wonder for a moment if he might just kill her anyway.

"Natalya is quite right, young man," Furan said. "Now why don't you all lay down your weapons and move over to the far side of the training area and allow us to leave? That is the only way that any of you are going to make it out of here alive."

"You expect me to believe that, Furan?" Raven yelled. "The minute you're safely out of here you'll trigger the device."

"Oh, my poor dear little Raven," Furan said. "That's your problem, you see. As long as I have this trigger I hold all the cards and you really have no alternative but to trust me."

Behind her the elevator from the upper levels pinged

and the prototype walked toward her, buttoning up his suit jacket.

"Good work with Malpense," Furan said. "A little over-dramatic perhaps, but it certainly made a point. Where is Heinrich?"

"He's on his way," the prototype replied. "He's purging the datacore."

"Well, he needs to hurry up. This is going to be a very bad place to be in a couple of minutes. Stay out of sight—I don't want anyone reporting your existence back to Nero."

The prototype simply nodded and Furan turned back to Raven.

"So, what is it to be, Natalya?"

Down on the training floor Raven's mind raced—they were rapidly running out of options. She glanced at Otto's body, lying just a few yards away, trying to ignore his staring lifeless eyes.

"Okay," Raven yelled back at her. "Let these students you have held hostage go and I will not harm you or your guards."

"Now why on earth would I do that, Natalya?" Furan shouted back at her.

"Because, if you do, I will surrender to you and you may do whatever you wish to me," Raven replied. "You'll still have the kill-switch to ensure my cooperation."

"No!" Shelby gasped. "She'll kill you."

"She'll kill all of us if I don't," Raven said quietly. "Don't worry, I can look after myself."

A smile spread across Furan's hideous, scarred face.

"An offer that is simply too delicious to refuse, Natalya," she said. "I accept."

"I want to know they're safe before I surrender to you," Raven said. "We have people on the surface. I won't give myself up to you until I know they're safe."

"Very well, they may use the elevator to travel to the upper levels. From there they must make their own way to the surface. I'm sure one of your clever little infiltrators there can show them the way," Furan replied. "The Darkdoom boy stays though." She pointed at Nigel. "To ensure your cooperation."

Raven glanced at Nigel and he gave a quick nod, swallowing nervously.

"Agreed," Raven said.

"Disengage the security checks on the elevator and open the main door," Furan said, turning to the prototype standing in the shadows behind her. He nodded and closed his eyes for a moment.

"Are you sure about this?" Wing said, his face set in a determined expression, but Raven knew him well enough by now to know when he was barely holding it together.

"Yes, don't worry, Wing," she said, putting a hand on his

shoulder. "I need your help now. You and Shelby have to get the others out of here as quickly and safely as possible."

Wing stared at her for a moment and then gave a tiny, almost imperceptible nod.

"Kill that witch," Shelby said, tears rolling down her cheeks, "for Otto."

"She's not getting away this time," Raven said, "trust me."

Shelby and Wing made their way over to the staircase leading up to the elevator with the rest of the captured H.I.V.E. students following closely behind them. A few minutes later Raven watched as the last of them boarded the elevator and slowly ascended toward the exit. Furan walked down the stairs, holding the kill-switch out in front of her, flanked by her men, all with their rifles pointing at Raven. Raven kept her own weapon levelled at Furan.

"And so, Natalya," Furan said, "once again, it is just you and me."

☻☻☻

Wing and Shelby were just finished ushering the last of the captured Alphas into the elevator leading up to the Glasshouse's entrance when a familiar voice came from behind them.

"You weren't thinking of leaving without me, were you?" Laura said.

Shelby spun around and saw her friend walking slowly

258

down the balcony toward them. She ran toward her and hugged Laura tight, tears of relief rolling down her face.

"You know we would never leave without you," Wing said. "We were just about to come back for you and Nigel."

"God, it's good to see you," Shelby said. "Are you okay?" She held Laura by the shoulders and inspected her face. She was pale and thin and there was a slightly haunted look to her eyes. Something about her was different, somehow she was not the same girl that Shelby had last seen all those months ago.

"I'm fine, but we have to get out of here," Laura said. "I don't have time to explain, but if Otto's plan doesn't work we're in big trouble."

"Oh, Laura, honey," Shelby said, her voice trembling suddenly. "I don't want to have to tell you this now, but Otto's dead."

"No, he's not," Laura said. "The person you saw fall wasn't Otto."

Shelby looked at her friend with a frown, suddenly worried that her mind might be more damaged than she had realized.

"Laura, it *was* Otto," Shelby said, shaking her head. "We all saw him."

"I'm sorry, Laura," Wing said. "Shelby is right. There is no doubt."

"Just listen to me," Laura said. "That wasn't Otto. It was a duplicate of him, a clone of some sort called Zero. Otto is down there right now with Furan, but she doesn't know it's him. He's going to try to disable the kill-switch."

"You know how crazy that sounds, right?" Shelby said.

"Of course, I do," Laura replied. "But crazy is what we do, remember. Otto's trying to buy us enough time to get everybody clear in case he can't disable the switch."

"Then we have to go and help him," Wing said, feeling a sudden surge of hope. "With our suit helmets on we should be safe from the gas, even if Furan releases it. We might be able to save him."

"No," Laura said, "you don't understand, Wing. That's what we discovered when Otto interfaced with the security system. Furan modified the design. The kill-switch doesn't release gas, it fills this whole facility with fuel vapor and then ignites it. It turns the Glasshouse into the largest fuel air bomb ever built. If he can't disable the switch this place will go up like a nuclear bomb."

"We still have to try and help him," Wing said.

"What we have to do is trust him, Wing," Laura said. "He's counting on us to get everyone to a minimum safe distance and if we're going to do that, we have to go now. Think, what would he tell you to do?"

"Get everyone to safety," Wing said with a nod.

"Exactly," Laura said, putting a hand on his shoulder.

Behind them the elevator doors opened and Franz stepped out, looking worried.

"The *Leviathan* is on its way to the collection point," Franz said. "I am needing help guiding the other Alphas through the minefield safely." He looked at the three of them with a frown. "I am so glad you are being safe, Laura, but where is Nigel?"

"He's on his way, Franz," Shelby said, "but right now, we have to get the hell out of here."

☻ ☻ ☻

"We're out," Shelby's voice crackled in Raven's ear. "*Leviathan*'s on its way in for pickup."

"Let the boy go," Raven said, nodding toward Nigel, standing nearby.

"Allow my men to restrain you without resistance and I'll let him leave," Furan said calmly.

Raven stood there for a moment, as if weighing her options before lowering her rifle and throwing it to the ground. Slowly she raised her hands in surrender.

"I'm not stupid, Natalya," Furan said. "The swords too, throw them away."

Raven slowly drew the twin katanas from the crossed sheaths on her back and tossed them across the floor toward Furan with a clatter.

"You, cuff her," Furan said to the man standing on her

261

left. He advanced cautiously toward Raven, pulling a set of restraints from a clip on his belt. He walked behind her and brought her hands down behind her back, cuffing them together.

"On your knees," the guard said.

"Now, let him go," Raven said with a nod toward Nigel as she lowered herself to the ground.

"Oh, I don't think so, Natalya," Furan said with a smile. "He's far too valuable for that."

"I'm sorry, Nigel," Raven said. She had known it was unlikely that Furan would honor her end of the deal, but the harsh truth was that it might have been enough to buy the freedom of the other captives. She could only hope that Diabolus would forgive her.

A couple of Furan's guards went over and grabbed Nigel as Furan walked toward Raven.

"And now, my dear, you're going to tell me everything you know about G.L.O.V.E., Nero, and his precious school," Furan said with a smile.

"You of all people should know I'll tell you nothing," Raven said.

"Oh, you will," Furan said, beckoning someone from the shadows nearby.

Raven's eyes widened in surprise as she recognized the boy in the dark suit.

"Otto!" she gasped. "But that's impossible."

"Oh, this isn't Malpense, Natalya," Furan said. "This is my version of him. An improved second draft, shall we say. We call him the prototype and he's going to reach inside that pretty head of yours and take everything from you. Only then, when you have betrayed everything you care about, will I kill you."

Raven looked at the corpse lying on the floor just a few yards away from her and then back at the perfect duplicate that was walking up behind Furan.

"You think that's an improved version of Otto?" Raven asked. "Well, I'll give you two reasons why you're wrong. Firstly, Otto was cleverer than any copy you could possibly create and secondly, he has blue eyes."

Furan felt the muzzle of a pistol press into the back of her skull.

"You know what they say—a copy's never as good as the original," Otto said, as Furan's men leveled their guns at him. Otto moved slightly to keep Furan between them and himself. "Now, tell your men to drop their weapons and release Nigel and Raven or I'll remove everything inside *your* head."

"Oh, well played, Mr. Malpense," Furan said, "but I fear that you are not quite as good a gambler as you think." She held up the kill-switch. "You know as well as I do that I'm holding the winning hand. This device is shielded against your abilities, as you've no doubt realized by now.

You kill me and we all die and there's not a thing you can do to stop it."

"Oh, you're quite right," Otto said, putting his free hand on her shoulder, "that trigger is shielded, but you're not."

Otto reached out with his abilities, using every last iota of the new power he had felt unlocking within himself since he had cracked the Disciple's encryption. Time seemed to suddenly slow to a crawl, he could feel the electrical impulses traveling through Furan's nervous system, flickering at the edge of his awareness. He felt her arm, as if it was his own, for the briefest instant, and suddenly he knew how Zero had been able to do what he did. He ordered the nerves in Furan's hand to contract the muscles into an iron grip and her hand clenched. Furan felt the horrible sensation of losing control of her own body as she realized that she could not release the trigger, even if she wanted to.

"Kill them!" Furan screamed. "Kill them all!"

Her men raised their rifles just as a white blur dropped toward them at phenomenal speed from overhead. Wing's adaptive forcefield generator fired with a deep, almost subsonic thump, cushioning his landing amongst Furan's men and sending them flying in all directions. He leaped to his feet, scooping up one of Raven's swords from the ground and engaging the crackling energy field that ran along its edge. Raven turned her back to him and he sliced through the cuffs binding her wrists with one clean swing, tossing the sword to her as she whirled back around to face him. One of the guards scrambled to his feet and Raven cut him down as Wing sent another flying with a kick to the chin. Raven picked her other sword up from where it had fallen and sprinted toward the other stunned guards as they staggered to their feet. A few seconds later, they were back on the ground, but this time they would not be getting up again.

As Raven finished her men, Furan lunged toward Otto, taking advantage of his focus on controlling her grip on the trigger. She twisted the pistol in his hand and he gave a pained yell as she wrenched it from him. As Raven and Wing turned toward her she spun around behind him, the hand that was holding the trigger snaking around his throat, her forearm crushing his windpipe as she pressed the pistol to his temple.

"Don't move," Furan yelled at them both.

"Give it up, Furan," Raven said, walking toward her, the blades of her katanas crackling. "It's over."

Furan tried to release the trigger on the kill-switch, but her hand still would not obey her.

"You think I'll let you take me alive?" Furan said. "You should know me better than that, Natalya. No, today I die and so do you."

She pressed the pistol hard into the side of Otto's head and squeezed the trigger.

A hundred yards above her Franz did exactly the same thing.

The neural shock pulse hit Furan square in the center of her forehead. Otto gasped as he felt her grip go slack around his neck, grabbing her hand as she fell and holding it firmly closed around the kill-switch.

Far above them Franz watched through the scope as Raven, Wing, and Nigel ran over to Otto, Raven pulling a field dressing from a pouch on her armor and using it to strap Furan's hand closed around the trigger. He let out a long deep breath.

"That's for kidnapping my friends."

chapter thirteen

Nero watched as Furan's unconscious body was carried up the *Leviathan*'s loading ramp on a stretcher, the kill-switch still bound tightly within her hand.

"Secure her for transport to H.I.V.E.," Nero said to the crewmen carrying the stretcher. "I'll deal with her later."

He walked down the ramp as Otto, Raven, Wing, Nigel, and Franz headed over toward the giant aircraft resting on the ice.

"Well done," Nero said. "I could not have asked for more from any of you."

"You have Franz to thank," Otto said with a smile. "We'd all be dead without him."

"It is being the lucky shot," Franz said with a dismissive wave of the hand.

"There was nothing lucky about it," Raven said.

Laura and Shelby were waiting for them inside the cargo bay as they walked up the loading ramp.

"See, I told you they'd all make it back in one piece," Shelby said as Wing came up to her and hugged her.

"Am I forgiven?" Wing asked.

"'Course you are," Shelby said. "I didn't mean what I said back there."

"So you don't think I'm a . . . what was it . . . suicidal idiot anymore?" he asked with a smile.

"Oh, you're still an idiot," Shelby said with a grin, "but I forgive you for being one. Anyway, all you had to do was free-fall inside a building—me and Laura had to get this lot through a minefield." She jerked her thumb over her shoulder toward the rescued Alphas who were milling around the far end of the cargo bay, looking excited, tired, and confused in equal measure. "That was fun."

"I'll bet," Otto said. He put a hand on Laura's shoulder. "How are you feeling?"

"Okay, under the circumstances," she said. "All I really want to do is get away from this place and never come back."

"Nigel!" Diabolus Darkdoom strode across the deck and embraced his son. "I was afraid I had lost you."

"I thought it was probably my turn to come back from the dead," Nigel said with a grin. "It is a family tradition after all."

"Indeed it is," Darkdoom said. "I'm told that I have you to thank for Nigel's safe return, Franz."

"Oh, it was being nothing really," Franz said.

"Nonsense," Darkdoom said. "I see a bright future for you, Mr. Argentblum. The Darkdoom family always repays its debts. Come on, you two, let's head up to the command center and you can tell me exactly what happened."

As he led the two boys away, the loading ramp began to whirr shut behind them and the Alphas at the other end of the bay began strapping themselves into the flight seats that lined the walls, ready for takeoff.

"Come on," Otto said to Laura, "we better get buckled up. Who knows what the range is on that transmitter that Furan's holding. Could be a bumpy ride."

"I'll be with you in a second," Laura said, as she saw Raven heading toward the stairs to the command center. She caught up with her and tapped her on the shoulder.

"Yes, Miss Brand," Raven said. "What can I do for you?"

"Doctor Nero just told me what you did," Laura said. "I wanted to thank you for saving my parents and my baby brother."

"You're welcome," Raven said with a nod. "Family should not be dragged into these things."

Outside, the *Leviathan*'s massive turbines powered up, blasting snow and chunks of ice in all directions as it slowly lifted into the air. As it roared away into the dawn sky the transmitter strapped into Furan's hand reached the limit of its range. Inside the silent abandoned halls of the Glasshouse, hidden nozzles began to spray a fine mist of jet fuel into the air. For a few seconds the cloud of noxious vapor hung in the air, filling every room and corridor and then the security network sent its final command and a sparking red flare dropped from the base of the glass spire at the heart of the facility. A split second later, the Glasshouse was gone, consumed by an explosion that would have been visible for miles around, if there had been a single living soul to see it.

☻☻☻

"Do you know why he wants to see us?" Laura asked.

"No idea," Otto replied. The fact of the matter was that when you were summoned to Nero's office you came. They'd been back at H.I.V.E. for barely more than twenty-four hours and, while the reappearance of the captured Alpha students had caused the rumor mill to start operating at full capacity, nothing else had happened that would explain why Nero wanted to see just the two of them. The door to Nero's office hissed open.

"Come in," Nero called out.

Otto followed Laura into the room and Nero gestured for the pair of them to sit in the chairs opposite him.

"Good morning, Miss Brand, Mister Malpense," Nero said. "I hope you have both had enough time to recover from your experiences in the Arctic."

"Yes, thank you, Doctor Nero," Laura said. "It's good to be back."

"I'm interested to hear you say that," Dr. Nero said, "because that's part of the reason I have asked you here today, Miss Brand. You're back in your uniform, I see." He gestured to the matching black Alpha stream jumpsuits that they were both wearing.

"Yes," Laura replied, "it's a relief to be honest after wearing the Glasshouse uniform for the past few months."

"That's good to hear," Nero said, "but the reason I called you in here today was to ask you a question. One that I do not ask lightly. Do you wish to continue to wear the uniform?"

"I'm sorry," Laura said, looking confused, "I'm not sure I understand."

"I mean, Miss Brand, I am prepared to offer you something that I have only offered to a handful of students over the years. If you wish, given what you and your family have been through at the hands of Anastasia Furan, I will allow you to leave H.I.V.E. without consequence and return home. That offer would, of course, be entirely dependent on you understanding that if you, or your family, ever breathed a word about the school to anyone there would be *consequences*."

"I . . . I'm not sure," Laura said. "I mean, I don't know, I'd have to think about it."

"Of course," Nero said. "You must understand two things though. Firstly, if you leave you will never be able to come back. Equally, if you decide to stay, then just like the rest of your fellow students you will be expected to complete your education before returning to the outside world. This is very much a one-time-only offer."

Laura said nothing, and just nodded.

"Secondly, and this goes for both of you, if you ever do anything to betray this school ever again, whether intentionally or not, I will have you both thrown to the sharks, no matter what I may or may not owe you. The only thing that has saved you both from that fate already is that I believe you honestly had no idea what the consequences would be when you stole the location of the Hunt and passed it on to a third party. That and the fact that it was only through your combined actions that we were able to rescue the surviving Alpha stream students are all that stayed my hand. Do I make myself *perfectly* clear?"

"Yes, sir," they replied in unison.

"Good," Nero said, as the door to his office opened again and Raven walked in. "I leave you to make your decision. I expect an answer within twenty-four hours. Natalya, would you escort Miss Brand to the communication center—there is one more thing I would like her to see before she makes her decision."

Laura stood up and followed Raven out of the room. Otto felt his heart sink as he saw the look on her face. He feared that he already knew what her decision would be. He got up to leave.

"I need to speak to you about something else, Otto. Please remain seated."

The door to his office closed and Nero got up from his chair, walking over to the fireplace that was carved into the rock wall, above which hung a portrait of a woman that Otto did not recognize, but who he had always been curious about.

"I listened to the recordings of your initial report," Nero said, turning to face him. "There were elements of it that were extremely disturbing, to say the least. You mentioned that the boy called Zero hinted that there were more clones like him somewhere."

"I can't be certain," Otto said, "but he kept referring to 'we' and 'us.' At first I thought he was talking about me and him, but I think there was more to it than that. Can I ask you a question?"

"Of course," Nero replied.

"Did you ever find the facility where I was born?"

"No, unfortunately, I'm afraid that was a secret that died with Overlord," Nero replied. "Why do you ask?"

"Because Furan mentioned that they were re-creating his work," Otto said, "and to do that they would, I'm sure, need access to the original lab. Professor Pike once told me that there was no way that the device inside my head could be manufactured with current technology. He said that it was a computer that would have to be grown, not built, and that we were decades away from even being able to attempt it."

"So you think the Disciples are using the technology that Overlord developed?" Nero said, frowning.

"Yes, but that's not what really frightens me," Otto said. "What frightens me is that I don't think they have the faintest idea what they're creating. I think they're tinkering with Overlord's technology without fully understanding it. Zero was, physically speaking at least, the same age as me, which implies that they're accelerating the growth of these clones. That's why they're not absolutely perfect copies of me, why Zero's eye color was wrong, for example. Those aren't the defects we need to worry about though. The defects we need to worry about are up here." Otto tapped the side of his head. "I was brought up like a normal child. I've always wondered why Overlord would do that. Why didn't he just keep me in a cage somewhere until he needed me? Perhaps he knew something that the Disciples don't—that something goes wrong if people like me, with my abilities, don't mature naturally."

"You're suggesting that they would turn out like this Zero character?"

"Exactly," Otto said. "I was barely able to survive an encounter with one of them. Normal people would be powerless to oppose them. If there are more of them out there, they could be the most dangerous foes we've ever faced. We have to find that lab, wherever it is, and shut it down. We have to shut it down *now*."

☢ ☢ ☢ ☢

Laura followed Raven through H.I.V.E.'s communication center, which was filled with technicians working on screens and talking into headsets. There was a large screen at the far end with a flattened map of the Earth displayed on it covered in red dots. Arcs were traced over these dots, plotting the trajectories of satellites as they orbited the planet. At any other time Laura would have been itching to get her hands on some of the technology in the room, but at that precise moment her mind was still reeling, trying to fully comprehend the offer that Nero had just made to her.

"In there," Raven said, gesturing to a small darkened room with a single seat in it. "I'll be right here. You have ten minutes."

Laura sat down in the seat with a confused frown as Raven closed the door behind her. A few seconds later a large high-definition screen flared into life just a couple of yards in front of her with the G.L.O.V.E. globe and fist logo in the center of it. Beneath the logo was the single word: Connecting . . .

She waited for a moment and then the screen flickered before resolving into the image of her parents, Mary and

275

Andrew Brand. Laura gasped as she she saw them and the baby that her mother was cradling.

"Laura, darling," her mother said, bursting into tears and reaching out to touch the screen. Laura touched her mother's hand and she too began to cry.

"Laura, honey, are you okay?" her father said, fighting to control his emotions like a good Scotsman and putting an arm around his wife. "They told us that something bad had happened to you. Are you safe now?"

"Yes," Laura said, regaining her composure with a sniff. "I'm fine, don't worry. Are you all okay?"

"Aye," her mother said, "though we wouldn't have been if it weren't for that woman called Raven. She saved us from those awful men who kidnapped us, and took us somewhere safe. I'm not supposed to say where we are."

"It's okay, Mom," Laura said. "Don't worry. You can trust her—the people who are protecting you are the same people who are training me."

"Is this the school that the Raven lady told us about?" her father asked. "I probably shouldn't have said that—she told us it was a secret and everything."

"It is, but I don't think she'll mind you telling me," Laura replied with a smile. She looked at the baby who was staring at the screen with obvious fascination. "Hello, little brother." She fought to hold back the tears again as he smiled back at her.

"This is Dougie," her mom said, picking up his tiny hand and waving it at her. "Your dad thinks he looks like him, of course, but I think he looks just like you. I can't believe how much you've grown. When you left you were still my little girl, but now you . . . you're a young woman."

Her mother started to cry again and Laura struggled to hold back her own tears.

"Aye," Laura said. "I've grown up a bit since then, Mom."

"Laura, I just wanted to say we're sorry," her father said. "When that man came to the house three years ago and told us that you had to leave with him or be arrested . . . we didn't want to do it, but he told us you could be facing twenty years in prison. He showed us the proof, he played us a recording of a conversation between the Americans and MI6. They turned up the next day. If we hadn't let them take you . . ."

"Dad, it's okay," Laura said. "I'm fine. I understand what you did. I admit, it took me a while to understand it and this place took a bit of getting used to, but I've got friends here and I'm being trained to do amazing, unbelievable things. I just miss you, that's all."

"We miss you too, darling," her mother said. "We just want the best for you, as long as you know that."

"Of course, I do, Mom," Laura said. "Now tell me all about wee Dougie."

A few minutes later Laura walked out of the room and Raven walked up to her and placed a hand on her shoulder.

"You okay?" Raven asked.

"I'm fine," Laura said with a sad smile. "Promise me one thing."

"What?"

"You'll keep them all safe, won't you? Whatever happens."

"Of course I will," Raven replied.

"Then that's all I need."

⚘ ⚘ ⚘

Robert Flack walked back into his office followed by Agent Simons.

"Well, that was unpleasant," Flack said with a sigh as he sat down behind his desk.

"I take it the President wasn't very happy," Simons said.

"I think that might be something of an understatement," Flack said, removing his glasses and rubbing the bridge of his nose. "Apparently he had to agree to attend one of the Italian Prime Minister's parties to apologize for the mess we caused in Venice."

"Oh dear," Simons said, sitting down opposite Flack with a manila folder in his lap.

"Apparently the first lady's even more unhappy about that than the President," Flack said, "and when she's unhappy heads are known to start rolling. Tell me you've got something that's going to brighten up my day."

"Maybe," Simons said. "What do you want first—the good news or the bad news?"

"Bad news, Simons," Flack replied. "You always lead with the bad news."

"Okay." Simons pulled an image of Darkdoom captured from the Italian CCTV footage from the folder. "We've drawn a blank on this guy. Our only lead was the MI6 link, but the Brits gave us nothing. Whatever they know about him, they're not sharing. In fact, and this might sound a little weird, the guy I spoke to at Vauxhall Bridge, well, he sounded nervous when I pressed him."

"So much for the Special Relationship," Flack said with a frown. "Tell them we'll remember how helpful they were next time they need a drone strike. Okay, what else?"

"Okay, slightly better news." Simons pulled an image of Raven from the folder.

"Aaah, our ghost," Flack said. "Tell me you have something on her."

"No name I'm afraid, but we ran her through the full archive—took a while obviously, and we found this." He handed Flack a memory stick, which he plugged into his laptop. On the screen there was security-camera footage of the woman in the photo talking to an older man. They were standing by a railing overlooking a city.

"Is that Rio?" Flack asked.

"Yup," Simons replied. "Keep watching."

Flack watched as the man and the woman exchanged a few words and then the woman threw something to the ground and the pair of them were obscured by a cloud of billowing smoke. When the smoke cleared the woman was gone and the man was standing on his own looking bewildered, with the bodies of six armed men lying on the ground around him.

"I remember this," Flack said, "the terrorist attack on the statue of Christ the Redeemer."

"Yeah," Simons replied, "except it wasn't a terrorist attack. That was just the story that was fed to the press. It was a failed hit and our ghost was the target. She took out the hitters and got clean away."

"So she's a professional," Flack said.

"Certainly looks that way," Simons replied.

"Who's the guy she's meeting?"

"That is one Esteban Guttierez," Simons replied. "He was taken in for questioning following the incident, but he claimed that he did not know the woman and that she was a complete stranger."

Flack rewound the recording to the moment that the woman and the man first met and froze the frame on the man giving the woman an affectionate hug.

"Sure look like friends to me," Flack said. "We have a lead on this Guttierez guy?"

"He vanished shortly after the incident," Simons replied.

"Someone take him out?"

"I don't think so," Simons said, shaking his head. "This

guy was a freelance contractor. Specialized in resolving *difficult* situations."

"We ever use him?" Flack asked.

"Yeah, couple of times during the eighties and nineties," Simons said. "I think he might have arranged his own disappearance."

"Okay, let's find him and pull him in," Flack said. "At this point he's the only lead on this woman and I think she's a major player. Anything else on the girl they met in St. Mark's Square? The one they pulled out of the canal."

"No, nothing," Simons said. "It's like she didn't exist before she attended architectural college. Wherever she was before that, she was under the radar."

"I don't like this, Simons," Flack said. "There are too many unanswered questions and I'm getting sick of telling the President 'we don't know.'"

"There is one piece of good news," Simons said, handing him the final piece of paper from the folder. "The forensics boys have been working on some of the documents we managed to pull from the building that blew up in Venice just before the incident in the canals. We still have no idea who the building belonged to. We've got guys on it, but you know what the Italians are like. However, we managed to get a pretty clear image reconstruction from one of the burned documents."

He laid an image of a badly burned schematic on the

table. It looked like the cross-section of a building hidden inside a mountain, but most of it was too badly damaged to make out. What he could make out was a single word in the bottom left-hand corner that was just legible.

"Okay," Flack said, "what the hell is H.I.V.E.?"

☣ ☣ ☣

Nero watched as the ground crew prepped the *Leviathan* for takeoff, the engineers rushing around the giant aircraft, detaching fuel lines and checking diagnostic readouts on their tablet displays. The large double doors at the top of the stairs leading down to the pad rumbled apart and Darkdoom and Nathaniel walked into the giant cavern. One of the flight crew ran up to Darkdoom and offered him his tablet which he scanned as Nero's father walked down the stairs toward him.

"Well," the old man said with a smile, "time to be off. Thank you for your hospitality, Maximilian. I'm glad that your rescue mission was a success."

"We wouldn't have been able to do it without you," Nero replied. "You're sure I can't persuade you to take a more active role in G.L.O.V.E. again?"

"Oh yes, quite sure. This is a young man's game, Maximilian," Nathaniel said with a dismissive wave of his hand.

"What are we both doing still playing it then?" Darkdoom said with a grin as he approached.

"I often wonder that myself," Nero said. "You will keep him out of trouble, won't you?"

"Oh, I'm sure that Diabolus can look after himself," Nathaniel said.

"I was talking to Diabolus," Nero said, raising an eyebrow.

"Of course," Darkdoom said, "you know I'm committed to caring for the homeless."

"Oh, very funny," Nathaniel said, hitting Darkdoom in the leg with his stick. "Less of your cheek, young man, or I might just contact young Nigel's mother and tell her exactly where he's been for the past few months. I understand you kept it from her. I wonder how she'd react to the truth?"

"Given the choice between the Disciples and my ex-wife," Darkdoom said with a sigh, "I'll take the Disciples. Rather less dangerous."

"Do you have any plans to set up a new office?" Nero asked Nathaniel as they made their way over to the *Leviathan*.

"In time, yes," Nathaniel said with a nod, "but it will take a while to find or build the right place, so in the short term I'm taking Diabolus up on a rather intriguing offer."

"Really," Nero said, "and what might that be?"

"A new *Megalodon*," Darkdoom said, "except bigger and better."

"This is what happens when someone doesn't have enough toys as a child," Nero said, rolling his eyes.

"It's really quite an ambitious project," Nathaniel said. "Not quite my usual thing, but it should be fascinating to work on."

"Why do I get the feeling that you two working together is going to end up causing trouble?" Nero sighed.

"No sense of adventure this one, Diabolus," Nathaniel said, pointing his stick at Nero. "That's always been his problem."

"I'd better get onboard and make sure that all the pre-flight checks are complete," Darkdoom said, as they reached the bottom of the *Leviathan*'s landing ramp.

"Thank you for your help, Diabolus," Nero said, offering his hand to his friend. "I won't let anything like that happen to Nigel again."

"I know that, Max," Darkdoom said, shaking Nero's hand. "Furan may be out of the picture, but the Disciples are still out there and they're just as dangerous as ever. I can't think of anywhere Nigel would be safer than right here." Darkdoom gestured at the rocky walls of the cavern. "See you soon, old friend."

Nero and Nathaniel watched Darkdoom walk up into the belly of the *Leviathan*.

"Good-bye, Maximilian," Nathaniel said, putting his hand on Nero's shoulder. "I'm sorry that we have not spoken more in recent years—we should rectify that in future."

"We should," Nero said with a nod.

"Anyway, mustn't keep Diabolus waiting," Nathaniel said, turning and heading up the loading ramp. He was halfway to the top when he stopped and turned around. "Your mother would have been very proud of what you've built here, Max. You should be too." Nathaniel turned and walked up into the cargo bay and the loading ramp whirred shut. Nero retreated to the entrance stairs as the *Leviathan*'s engines roared into life and the huge hangar doors that sealed off the crater above slowly began to rumble open. Nero watched the *Leviathan* slowly lift off the pad.

"I hope you know what you're letting yourself in for, Diabolus," Nero said to himself with a wry smile. "I really do."

☣☣☣

Otto sat, lost in thought, on a sofa in a quiet corner of the library with a book sitting unread on his lap. He always retreated there when he wanted time to think in peace and he had a lot to think about at the moment. He hadn't really spoken to anyone about how deeply his encounter with Zero had disturbed him. After Sebastian Trent had used the Animus fluid to control him and turn him against his friends, Otto had always sworn that he would never let anyone do that to him again. With the destruction of Overlord he had thought that maybe the threat that he might lose control again was finally gone, but Zero had used him like a puppet. The thought of there being more clones like him out there terrified him. That wasn't the only thing that was bothering him though. He was just as concerned about the offer that Nero had made to Laura, purely because he was ninety percent certain he knew exactly what her decision would be. His Blackbox, the device that H.I.V.E. gave to all pupils to use as a combined communicator and PDA, vibrated in his pocket and Otto pulled it out. A moment later the screen lit up with H.I.V.E.mind's face.

"Good afternoon, Otto," H.I.V.E.mind said. "I have completed the search of G.L.O.V.E. records that you requested. I found no reference to any facility that might have been used for the purpose you described."

"I didn't think you would," Otto said with a sigh. "That would have been too easy."

"There are many G.L.O.V.E. records that I also searched that I am not allowed to discuss with someone with your security clearance," H.I.V.E.mind said. "I am not allowed to tell you that those searches were also negative."

"Thanks," Otto said with a smile. "I appreciate it."

"I also thought you should know that I gave Miss Brand your current location two minutes and thirty-seven seconds ago," H.I.V.E.mind said. "She is currently one hundred and twelve yards from your location in corridor H-nine."

"Thanks for the warning," Otto said, taking a deep breath.

"Otto," H.I.V.E.mind said.

"Yeah," Otto replied, sounding slightly distracted.

"I have spent a great deal of time interfaced with your consciousness over the past few months. I will not begin to even pretend to understand the chaos and unpredictability that runs through the human mind at any given moment. Frankly, I am amazed that your species ever even learned to stand upright, let alone do all the astonishing things you have done whilst processing so much redundant data. However, one thing I have realized is that there is often a large differential between the things that you say and the things that you feel or truly believe. It is a peculiarly human trait."

"Is there a point to all this?" Otto said with a slight frown.

"Yes," H.I.V.E.mind replied with a nod. "I have processed all of the probability vectors and have calculated a mathematically optimum strategy. Tell her how you really feel."

Before Otto could reply, H.I.V.E.mind vanished from the screen.

"Hi, Otto," Laura said as she walked up behind him and pulled up a chair.

"Hey," Otto said with a smile, "how are you doing?"

"Better actually," Laura said. "It's been nice to have some time to actually think. You know, there was a time when I thought of this place as a prison. I think we all did, but the Glasshouse changed all that."

"I can imagine," Otto said.

"It's also made me think about the future," Laura said, looking at the floor, "about what comes after this. I don't know if I'm cut out for this."

Laura looked up from the floor and stared into his eyes for a second.

"I wanted to come and talk to you first," Laura said. "I've made a decision."

"I know," Otto said. "I don't blame you, Laura. I really don't. You've got a family, your baby brother, and after everything that Furan put you through . . . I love you, Laura, but I know you have to go. I want you to stay, of course, but—"

"Otto Malpense, I've said it before and I'll say it again, you may be the smartest kid in the room, but you can be unbelievably stupid sometimes." She leaned forward and kissed him. It felt just as perfect as he had always imagined it would. After a couple of seconds, she pulled away from him and smiled. "I'm staying, you idiot."

Otto felt a rush of overwhelming relief, a huge grin spreading across his face. He pulled her to him and kissed her again.

"Only these two would make out in the library," Shelby said.

Otto and Laura quickly separated, both turning interesting shades of crimson.

"I pleaded with Shelby to give you some privacy," Wing said with a sigh, looking slightly uncomfortable, "but I fear she does not have a great deal of respect for boundaries."

"Boundaries, schmoundaries, no way I'm missing the first Brand–Malpense smooch," Shelby said with a grin. "I've been waiting three years for this."

"Thanks, Shel," Laura said, shaking her head. "You're always such a big help in these situations."

"What situations are these being?" Franz asked as he and Nigel rounded the corner.

"We miss something?" Nigel asked.

"Did you sell tickets?" Otto said to Shelby with a frown.

"No, but you know, that's actually not a bad idea," Shelby replied.

"I was just telling Otto that Doctor Nero has told me that I can keep my place at H.I.V.E.," Laura said.

Otto didn't say anything. For whatever reason, Laura obviously didn't want the others to know about the choice that Nero had given her. It was her decision and he wasn't going to argue with it.

"That is fantastic news, Laura," Wing said, giving her a quick hug. "It is good to have you back."

"He's just glad that Otto's got someone else to talk to about computers now," Shelby said, also hugging her friend. "Would have sucked to be here without you, hon."

On the other side of the library, Penny glanced over her

shoulder at the six of them. Her eyes narrowed for a moment, something cold and hard behind them. Then she turned and walked away.

☻☻☻

Nero walked down the bare rock corridor toward the steel door at the far end. He stood for a moment and waited as the scanner above the door swept a broad laser beam over him.

"Identity confirmed, welcome, Doctor Nero," a synthesized voice said. The door rumbled aside and a long metal walkway started to extend from the threshold, crossing the boiling lake of magma far below and connecting with another metal door on the other side of the chamber. The first door closed behind him and only then did the door in front of him open. He walked into the small room carved out of the rock wall and over to the clear panel of ten-inch-thick bulletproof glass that divided it.

"Hello, Anastasia," Nero said, as he approached the glass.

Furan turned to face him, dressed in simple white pajamas. The cell she occupied had a sink, a toilet, and a metal hatch in one wall. Other than that it was bare.

"Why didn't you just kill me, Nero?" Furan said, staring at him with a look of pure hatred.

"I don't believe in the death penalty for people like you, Anastasia," Nero said. "It's too lenient."

"So what *do* you intend to do with me?"

"Nothing," Nero said, "nothing at all. You see that's the worst possible punishment for people like us, Anastasia, irrelevance. You will die down here one day, alone and forgotten. Your mind will probably have gone by then, but, honestly, I don't care."

"Just finish this!" Furan screamed at him.

"I already have," Nero said. "Good-bye, Anastasia."

He turned and walked through the door.

"Nero, come back," Furan screamed. "Neeeerooooo–"

Her final scream was silenced as the door thudded shut.

☻☻☻

Dr. Klein attached the air hose to his biohazard suit and waited as the decontamination process ran its course, blasting him with jets of disinfectant steam. The jets deactivated and he walked down the corridor toward a pair of steel doors with the words "Project Absalom" printed above them and the barbed-wire circle logo of the Disciples carved into its surface. The doors hissed open as he approached and he went inside. One of the many scientists working all around the room approached him as he entered the laboratory.

"We heard about Furan's capture and the destruction of the Glasshouse," his assistant said. "Did the prototype survive?"

"It appears not," Klein said. "Though its performance up

until then was exemplary. Joseph Wright has taken command of the project. He's keen for us to press on with stage two."

"That's a relief," the other man said. "The accelerated maturation process appears to be working even more efficiently with the phase two subjects." The man handed him a digital tablet and Klein studied the data.

"Excellent. I shall inform Mr. Wright that we are ahead of schedule." He handed the tablet back to his assistant and walked through the lab. The room was filled with all manner of the latest cutting-edge scientific and medical hardware, equipment that any research institute would have given almost anything to assemble in one place like this. He inspected the large empty tank with the number zero printed on it. It was a shame that the prototype had been lost, but in truth it had largely served its purpose as a proof of concept. He walked to the far end of the lab and looked through the toughened glass window at the tanks that lined the wall in the refrigerated room beyond. In each tank was a floating body, currently the size of a toddler, but growing at a vastly accelerated rate. The tanks were each individually numbered from one to twelve. On the wall above the tanks there was a display counting down to the moment when they would have reached their full potential.

99 Days 17 Hours 8 Minutes 14 seconds

99 Days 17 Hours 8 Minutes 13 seconds

99 Days 17 Hours 8 Minutes 12 seconds . . .

Join the world's most talented villains for more incredible adventures at H.I.V.E. It would be criminal not to. . . .

Thirteen-year-old master criminal Otto Malpense has been chosen to attend H.I.V.E., the top-secret school of Villainy. But there's one small catch —he cannot leave until his training is complete. He's left with one option. Escape. He just needs to figure out how.

A new power is rising to challenge Number One, the most formidable villain alive. But who is it? And why do they want to assassinate Otto Malpense, star pupil of H.I.V.E., and his best friend, Wing Fanchu?

H.I.V.E. is in grave danger. Dr. Nero, its leader, has been captured by the world's most ruthless security force. It's up to Otto to save him, but first he must escape from Nero's sinister replacement.

One of the world's most powerful villains is threatening global Armageddon, and Otto, Wing, and his most trusted villain-friends find themselves in the sights of the most dangerous man alive, with nowhere to run.

Otto Malpense, star pupil at the top-secret school for Villainy, has gone rogue. In a deadly race against time, Raven and Wing must find Otto before the order to eliminate him can be carried out.

The evil A.I. Overlord is about to put his terrible plans into action. Then no one will be able to stand in his way. It is time to activate Zero Hour, a plan designed to eliminate any villain on the brink of global domination.

Otto and the rest of the elite Alpha stream have been sent on their most dangerous exercise yet: the Hunt. But when Otto and the Alphas arrive in the icy wastes of Siberia, it becomes clear that something is wrong. There's a traitor in their midst, and time is running out to discover who it is.